LOVE WILL
NEVER DO

LOVE WILL NEVER DO

NAKIA ROBINSON

Love Will Never Do

ISBN: 978-0-9890982-4-3

Dedication

This book is dedicated to John H. Fraling and
Robert Lee Robinson. Thank you for instilling
in me the quality of humility. Every day I live by
your words: "If I help someone along the way, then
my living shall not be in vain" & "It's nice to be
important, but it's more important to be nice."

Acknowledgements

Mommy – I love you. Thank you for being my rock and support. You continue to be that rare priceless jewel. Kidra, Renny and I, are so blessed to have you as our mother. Every day we hope to make you proud and let the world know our mother is Barbara Wawa. I work hard because I want you to rest. You need to be treated like the queen you are.

Antoine – My biggest promoter. I couldn't do it without you. You drive me crazy most of the time, but you inspire me to be greater. My children thank you again for allowing me the time needed to finish this project. I love you all.

Kidra and Renny – Thank you for being my inspiration. Queen, you are in a class of your own. Ms. Extraordinaire, you need no introduction, truly marvelous. How lucky I am to have a sister like you. Lil' Boy you have so many talents. Can't wait to see the business you grow. The best is coming.

Lyndon – It hasn't been a year and this is my third book. All possible because of you. I am so fortunate to have you on my side. You never steer me wrong. I have the utmost respect and admiration for you. You are a godsend. You make it happen. You are THE BEST. Thank you, thank you, thank you.

Jacci – Thank you. You know this mind of mine is crazy. Thank you for directing it to flow on paper. LOL! I must warn you, so many ideas I'm scared of what I might do next.

Natalie – Thank you again for working on my project. You are appreciated.

Chaundrae – A true hustler and motivator. I am so blessed to have you in my corner. Thank you for the late night and early morning calls. Your encouragement and support was needed. You need to write a book. You have a story to tell. I have a coach with connections that will make it happen. Until then, I look forward to seeing your business blossom.

My grandmothers – Thank you.

CF crew – Thank you for putting up with my many outbursts and encouraging me to pursue my dream. If my mouth was "uncensored" before, watch out. It's a part of the creative process. LOL!

Antoine "Inch" Thomas – Thank you for the genuine support. It's always a pleasure to talk with you. I gain so many valuable gems.

Mr. Larry – Thank you for being the first one to carry my books and your continued support.

My favorite couple, Cuz Tyronna and Fam – Love you. Thanks for promoting.

My cousin Michelle Greer – Thank you for your knowledge and guidance.

Source of Knowledge, Dexter George, and Patrice McKinney - Thank you. It is truly an honor to have you believe in me. Thanks again for the continued support.

Tyeisha and Dreas – Thank you for the sisterhood. True innovators. Can't wait for the world to see your talent.

Cretia, Cool Press, and Suga Mama – Thank you for cheering me on. It means so much.

BBBC (Bad Bitty Book Club) - Thank you having me at your meeting. You were my first and will forever hold a special place. You ladies are the best and a lot of fun. Looking forward to more meetings.

Readers and Book Clubs – Thank you for taking the time to read my book. I genuinely appreciate you. As always, I hope you will feel Landon's story and emotions. What a story she has....

–'the next piece !

Heaven Can Wait

He stares at me with so much hate. I know I deserve it but it hurts.

"You just think you can say sorry and all is forgiven?"

"I am sorry. I honestly never meant to hurt you."

"Shut the hell up!"

"I thought ... I - I - I wanted him to be yours," I stuttered.

"Landon, you ain't nothing but a gold-diggin' hoe. Tony told me to stay away from yo' ass! He said how you was nothin' but a high class escort. Trifling Bitch!" Then he slapped me across my face with so much force I thought my neck snapped. I swear he's trying to slap the skin off my face. I hold my stinging face while checking for blood.

"My career is over because of you! I'm a fucking joke! You fucked the damn league and even fucked my teammates in my house," he slaps me again just as hard as before.

"Eric, I swear I didn't fuck any of your teammates in your house," I pleaded. He returned a sinister laugh.

"I didn't."

He grabbed me and pushed me hard into the wall saying, "Bitch, you gonna look me in the face and still lie to me? Lie and tell me you ain't fuck anyone in my house and then smile in my face. You gonna stand here and tell me you ain't fuck nobody else while I was married to your trifling ass?"

I put my head down.

He yanks it up, hard, "Answer me bitch!"

His eyes are dark, nothing but pure hate for me; so much callous hate I caused. I close my eyes.

He grabs my face, "Open your goddam eyes and look at me!"

I admit I have done him dirty on so many levels. His anger and hurt is justified. I honestly didn't set out to hurt him. It was never my plan. I got caught up and I made one bad decision after another. Before I knew what happened or realized the magnitude of my actions, it was too late. I just did what I knew and rode the wave. Unfortunately, that wave was too big, too powerful, and I couldn't ride the tide.

"Landon! You hear me talking to you?" he slaps me again.

"You got a good laugh off of me, spent my money, and talked me like I was your puppet," another slap.

"Eric, I'm so sorry. I thought he was yours. I wanted him to be your son," I cried.

"You ain't nothing but a lying whore," he grabs me, yanking my neck. "Landon, I'm going to ask you this and your ass better not lie. Do you understand me?"

"Yes," I croak.

"Why did you kill my baby?"

I swallowed hard. I was too scared to answer him;

too scared to tell him the truth. I didn't want to tell him that I didn't know if the baby was his. I closed my eyes, debating whether or not I should tell him the truth, praying silence would be enough. Of course it wouldn't be.

He grabbed my jaws and said in a low chilling voice, "Open yo' mutherfucking eyes, look at me and answer my damn question."

I was so tired of the lies, so tired of the schemes and the running. I was tired of all this shit. I obey. I look him in the eyes as the tears roll down my face and respond, "I didn't know if you were the father."

He releases me. My words have his mind spinning as they set off a new war within him. He wanted me dead. He wanted me to pay. I shiver, scared to move, scared it would trigger him to act on his anger. Looking at him, I knew his mind was unraveling right before my eyes. . His mind was gone. My truths struck something deep within. I wanted to move, run, do something to get away, but I couldn't, my movement would snap him from the delusion and disbelief he was in and focus his attention back to me. I stood still, careful not to make a move or a sound.

He began to rock back and forth slowly and in a low shrill voice said, "You took my career, my money. Now you tellin' me you took TWO kids from me?"

The next thing I knew he came at me full force, grabbing me by the neck and throwing me against the wall. My head hit the wall hard and I fell to the floor like a rag doll. I lay against the cold marble with my tears soaking the floor.

Eric paces the floor, talking to himself. "I don't believe this shit. This bitch. I should've listened to Nana, now she gone. I don't have no kids. This bitch…kill her. I got to kill her. She got the whole league laughing at me. She gotta die. She took my kids. She took my kids."

My body tenses at the sound of his words.

Within seconds, he yanked me up in the air screaming, "Tell me why I should let you live!"

Sadly, I don't have any answers…no response.

"Just what I fucking thought! There *is* no reason. Your ass needs to die."

Tears run down my face, my chest heaves in and out, my legs ready to buckle.

Eric grabs my neck, I want to throw up, but nothing could come. His hands are sucking the air from me. They are muscular and strong from years of dribbling the basketball. My feet are barely touching my pretty marble floor. He squeezes tighter. My eyes bulge from the pressure. My face hot is hot, swelling from a lack of oxygen. He's killing me, slowly, painfully.

I squirm, struggling from being deprived from oxygen, knocking any and everything down. The thump from the photo frame snaps Eric from his trance. He looks at the photo, then he looks at me and immediately releases his grip as if the realization of what he is doing hits him.

I fall to the floor gasping for air, holding my burning chest. The tears burn my cheek and my head pounds. I need to move, lock myself in a closet, do something before he literally squeezes the life out of me. I try to focus, I try to move, but I'm paralyzed from pain, lack of oxygen. I look over to see Eric sitting on the floor, knees up holding a picture. He's crying. His eyes scream hurt, disbelief, so much pain. My pounding heart breaks, my body in so much pain, I'm barely able to breathe. But looking at him, I wish I could take all his pain…erase me from his memory. I feel so horrible in so many more ways as I look at him holding that picture.

I remember the day the picture was taken. It was little Eric's first birthday. My little baby loved me. He was my baby, but from the beginning Eric was more hands on with diapers and feedings. He was so proud. There were many days that I had spa days while they had father and son bonding days. I love my son, but Eric lived for him. He had just begun to walk. Lil' Eric grabbed a hunk of cake and took a bite. He lifted his little chubby arms to be picked up. I was not getting messy in my peach Prada romper, so Eric eagerly obliged, swooping him up in his arms. Lil' Eric tried to wrap an arm around Eric's neck while saying, "Ea... Dada, Ea... The photographer captured the moment of son feeding his father, his idol, cake. I always loved the innocence in my baby's eyes. The picture shows the adoration, the love he has for him. I recall the sweet memory and I hurt even more. I recall how after the photo was taken the photographer caught another of Eric kissing the son he thought was his and little Eric doing the same. It was a wonderful day; we were a family. The party, the cake fight afterwards, I wasn't even mad when they both smeared my pretty romper. It was all fun…but it was a lie.

Eric slowly gets up. I brace myself for more de-served pain. He stands over me, staring. He looks down at the photo, steps over me and then peacefully leaves out of the door with the photo in hand.

Oh my god, I feel so bad. Eric is so right, sorry would not change things. It would not erase the years he lost for being caught up in my lies. So much damage I've done. There was nothing I could do to make it right, being with me destroyed the man he was, turned him into a psychotic mess.

My life is a mess. Everything is closing in on me. The bitch called Karma has come back to take me out. Karma has many allies and too much ammunition. I don't have any fight left in me. So much has transpired in these last few weeks. I knew she would come back to make me suffer, break me down and leave me calling for death to rescue me.

My front door opens, I try to move, but my body is exhausted. Not sure how long I'd been down, I remained still, allowing the wetness of my tears to cascade across my marble floor. I don't look up until he steps in front of me. Dirty black steel toe boots are there.

"You thought I was playing with your ass!"

His voice is so powerful and menacing that my body trembles.

I don't move fast enough, the dirty black steel boots lift and come crashing down on my ribs. Then another kick to my stomach so severe and forceful, I slide to the other side of the room.

"I'm sorry," I cough and cry in agony.

"Sorry don't mean shit to me."

He grabbed my arm, pulling my 105-pound frame up like it was a mere fifteen pounds.

I wince from the pain.

He grabs my bruised neck and laughs, "You always liked it rough."

He holds my neck tight, but not tight enough to choke me. He taunts me instead.

"You were always a high price hoe who thought you were in charge. You thought you were a boss bitch. No, bitch! You were always a hoe. . An expensive overpriced hoe!"

I cry. .

"Pussy wasn't all bad, not the best. You served your purpose. For old time's sake, huh?"

I groan.

He laughs and pulls out his dick.

"No," I plead.

"If yo' ass knows what right, you better suck me dry and right. Now assume position."

I get on my knees. He walks up to me, his dick hard and ready.

"Suck my dick hoe. You never had a problem before. I give you your props. That tongue of yours was a great stress reliever. Like I said suck it right. I may have mercy on you."

I do as he requests sucking him for my life. He wasn't lying I'd done this many times before. I knew what to do to get him to release and within two minutes I was swallowing his sour cum.

He pulls out and smiles, "Damn, that was some good shit, but not enough for me to forget. Stand up."

I do. "I'm sorry. I was wrong," I babble.

"You damn right, you were wrong. You were a conniving hoe. You think I'm playing your ass. You think I'm just gonna let you play me? Bitch, you got me fucked up. Yo' ass is gonna pay."

"Please," I cried.

"Please what? Please don't hit you?" He smacks me, releasing his grip from my neck. "Please don't kick you?" He took his steel toe boot and kicked me in the back as I attempted to run. My knees buckled and I crashed down. I hear a pop in my right knee and pain immediately follows.

"Please don't do what?" His steel boot came down hard crashing into the side of my head. He stomped again, again, and again. I swear my ear rang, busted, and echoes began.

He was talking but I was in too much pain and his voice sounded so muffled. He grabs me, trying to stand me, but my knee was not allowing. I wobble. He pushes me up against the wall. My equilibrium off, I want to just fall to the floor, but I knew better.

"All the money you took from me. You think I'm going to take it as a loss?"

"You're right. I'm sorry. Give me a couple of days to liquidate some funds," I plead.

"Oh now you want to make arrangements," he laughs. "There are no more options."

"Please, please, please. I'm sorry."

"Please don't what, bitch?" He kicks me in the

stomach. If my body didn't absorb the blow, there would have been a hole in the wall.

I go down hard, coughing, mouth spewing blood.

He comes at me with no mercy at all. He continuously stomps on me. Each time, cracking bones

echo in my head, while the pain radiates throughout my body. . Boom, Boom, Boom, Boom, Boom

Boom!

He finally stops, but I have no relief.

"Get the fuck up, Landon."

"I can't," I moan.

"Bitch, I said get the fuck up!" He grabbed my yellow shirt, now stained with red blood, ripping it in the process propping me up like a mannequin. My right knee was swollen, unable to bend. I force my weight to my left leg.

I cry out from pain.

"Look at me, bitch!"

I look up in time to see fire. At the same time, I feel my chest burn. I grab my chest trying to alleviate the sting, the burn, but it only intensifies. My hands are slippery, soaked with blood. I feel water running down my legs, I had peed on myself. Everything is in slow motion as my knees buckle, but the crash on the floor stuns me with new pain.

I lie on the floor trying to inhale but my lungs are caving in on me. I need air. . My nose is running with blood making it impossible to breathe. I open my mouth gasping for air, but there too blood is running freely. Death is the easy solution, but I still have fight left in me.

I know a lot of people can't stand my ass. They probably think getting shot is justification for the wrongs that I've done. But death? I just want you to keep an open mind. There's always more, perception can go either way. You know facts, but you don't know my story. Hear me out before you rejoice and say I got what I deserved.

1

Break It Down

"Landon, baby. Mommy's here baby, fight. Mommy's here. Don't leave mommy. Please don't leave me baby. Fight baby."

"Jackie, let her go so the doctors can do their job!" Daddy pleads.

"Get the hell away from me Lawrence. She is my baby. She needs me."

"I know she does, but the doctors need to do their job. Jackie let them save her!" he yells with frustration.

"Fight, Landon! Keep pushing, just like I taught you. You are strong. You are gorgeous. You are strong. You are a survivor. Fight baby for mommy."

"Ma'am, please. Let us do what we need to do. We need to save your daughter."

"You better save my daughter. I want only the best surgeons. I don't care about the cost. Save my daughter!"

"Jackie!" my father yells.

"Only the best for my daughter! I don't want an intern. This is not a teaching session! No mishaps or I swear you will wish you were dead when I m done with you."

"Jackie, that's enough. Take her." I hear my father order the doctor.

"Stay strong, Landon!"

That's my mommy. I love her so much. She's taught me so much. She is the one who nurtured me, gave me the confidence I needed and made sure I never doubted my worth or beauty. My life has always been a façade that I became accustomed to living. It was the only thing I knew. Like I said before, perception can go either way. Many look at me and think I'm an arrogant snooty bitch. They think I'm nothing but a spoiled brat. I haven't a heart or soul. I'm conniving, ruthless and too demanding. Yes, I do, well, did have diva antics but it's only because I deserve respect and the arrogance everyone assumes was just pure confidence. I was taught I didn't need anyone to tell me what I was. I always knew I was gorgeous, smart, and strong, destined to be the best and have the best. I learned I control my destiny, if I didn't I would play the fool. But for Landon, being a fool was never an option.

I've seen what happens with a woman when she puts too much trust and love in a man. It's always been a double standard. Men want you to be devoted to them. Their logic is they gave you the ring, last name, so you should be honored to be put on that elite pedestal. While you are the first lady you will never be the only lady. Men marry you and in the beginning it's all lovely, we will live happily ever after. What happens next is either one of the following, boredom, temptation or greed. Men justify this by saying, "I was just fucking them girls, you the only one I want. I gave you the ring, my last name." You fight, scream, take away pussy privileges and within weeks, things are back to "normal" until next time. So they go out there, share the dick getting it worn out, take it to the next chick, bring it back to you and think you should be jumping for joy because you are the first lady. To add more insult, they brag and tell stories to their boys. Just like I don't want a used car with miles that's been through repairs, I don't want STD's. The more miles the more damage to the motor and once the motor gone the car or should I say, the dick is useless. You'll be waiting for a monthly Viagra prescription which will kill spontaneity. Then men want to be all up in their feelings if you go out and cheat. He'll be crying, saying you a hoe, trifling, damaged goods and next he'll be divorcing your ass. That double standard shit blows me. Landon never would be going with that program.

The reason for my logic and the cause of my attitude towards men began forming at the age of twelve. The first argument I can recall between my mommy and daddy. That argument changed my adoration for daddy.

"Lawrence, you need to keep your whores in check. I will not be disrespected. You're getting sloppy again."

I'll never forget the pain in her eyes and the tears falling as a result. She put on a good front, but standing was a scorned woman whose husband had betrayed her. I knew even then in some way or another daddy would pay. I stood on the spiral stairs watching their argument play out in the huge rectangular mirror.

"You got another bitch pregnant."

"Jackie, hear me out."

"What the hell can you say Lawrence? It was an accident. It didn't mean anything. You were set up?"

"No, that's not what I was going to say."

"What do you have to say Lawrence?" Mommy hisses.

"What evidence or proof do you have I impregnated another woman?"

"Lawrence, don't start that courtroom bullshit with me."

Daddy always appeared relaxed, in charge, right now was no different. He said unfazed, "Jackie, this is crazy. I did not get anyone pregnant."

"This time," she said sarcastically.

"Jackie, no one is pregnant. I had conversations with her regarding a case, but I never entered a sexual relationship with her."

"Really? You really insist on standing here in front of me lying. You don't think I did my research. You think I'm stupid and that I'm going to fall for this bullshit. Lawrence, at least be honest."

"Jackie, there's nothing to tell."

"Very good, Lawrence never break under pressure. You know what since you can't admit your indiscretions and since I don't feel like playing this game with you let me lay it on the table. Your naïve whore called to tell me you were in love with her." She pauses. "She then proceeds to tell me we are adults and we should come and discuss this. She tells me she understands how difficult it is for me to let go, but it's for the best."

Mommy picks up one of her law books and aims it at daddy. Daddy manages to duck and she hurls more books and only stops when one hits him between the eyes."

"Jackie, she's lying," he said holding his head.

"Lawrence, I told you I was not in the mood for this game!"

"Shh, you're going to wake Landon."

She throws another book at him that hits him in the chest. "The whore also insisted that she would make the transition for Landon as easy as possible and is dedicated to making this blended family work."

He walks over to Mommy to try to comfort her. "Jackie."

"Don't you dare touch me. Lawrence I've turned my back to a lot of shit, but this however crosses the line. Do not involve my child in your lies. Do not involve my child at all. Do you understand?"

Daddy doesn't speak.

"No defense."

"Jackie, I'm sorry. It was horrible judgment. She was a fling. I never meant to hurt you and she is very delusional. I'm dedicated to you. I love you."

"Shut the hell up, Lawrence."

"Jacqueline, I really do love you and Landon. "

"She knows my daughter's name. Seems like there was some pillow talk. Meaning it was more than a fling. Stop it!"

"Oh, Jackie."

"I will not be embarrassed. Call your whore now and put her on speakerphone. Confess you were using her. You will tell her it's over. Tell her how you lied and to never contact you again."

"Jackie really is all that necessary?"

"For a liar like you, yes."

Daddy did as mommy requested. The whore, as mommy called her, didn't take it well. She said her and daddy were supposed to be together and have a family. At that point mommy was done and told him to end the call. That's when she really broke down. She yelled, cried and told mommy he would be back because she couldn't satisfy him. Daddy told the crazy chick he was in love with mommy and to never disrespect her, which was funny. At 12, I knew better and had to laugh at the hypocrisy. He told her if she tried to harass his family or slander him in any way he would get a restraining order and sue.

Once the call was done, daddy tried to get into mommy's good graces.

"Jackie, I apologize for putting you threw that. It won't happen again. I am committed. I know I have a long road ahead of me in regaining your trust, but I promise I will. This was the only indiscretion I've had since our marriage. It will be the last."

"You forgot about that huge one13 years ago."

"Uh, we weren't married then."

"That's the best you could do?"

"Jackie."

"Lawrence, we need a break."

"I don't want to lose you."

"Now you want to communicate. I gave you the option earlier and you didn't take it."

"I didn't want to hurt you."

"You should have thought about that before you slid your dick in that whore."

"I'm willing to do whatever it takes to save our marriage." Daddy pleads.

Mommy gives him a vicious look. "You will leave this house now. I have a few cases to handle this week so I will be in the office. I advise you to stay as far away as possible. When I'm done, Landon and I will be taking a trip. While on the trip I will have Landon call you once a day. You miss the call that's your fault. Do not call me at all."

"Jackie, what will you tell Landon?"

"Oh, I won't tell her you're a lying cheating bastard. I will tell her you're away on business. When I leave, you can return."

"I need to see my daughter."

"You lied to your whore and the bitch had the nerve to tell me we can work out a joint custody agreement like she was running the show. You should have thought about that before you put that lie out there. Since you did, deal with it."

"Jackie, please let's not do this."

"The arrangement is I will have full custody of Landon. You will see her in three weeks after our trip."

"Where am I supposed to go this week?"

"I really don't care. You had no problem coming up with stories for the bitch. Figure it out."

"Jackie we can come up with some type of compromise."

"You closed that window of opportunity. You need to leave."

"What about us?"

"We are separated as of now. However, that doesn't mean I want to hear or see you with your little bitches. As far as this marriage, will I end it? I will be weighing my options."

"There is no one else. You are my wife, my partner, my love."

"Get the hell out of this house now, Lawrence."

"Alright Jackie, I will give you some space. I'm going to check in on Landon and then grab some things."

I tiptoed upstairs and slid in bed before daddy came in. Tears flowed loosely, I tried not to sniffle, tried to be strong, but I was devastated. Fortunately, mommy stopped him before he entered telling him I would want to know why he was leaving so late to do business. He must have rationalized that he shouldn't get in the habit of lying to his daughter.

Yup, daddy was the first man to break my heart. He was the hardest heartbreak and one I never got over.

*

During the following weeks, my talks with daddy were short and brief. Each time he tried to prolong the conversation, I would find any reason to get off the phone. One day, while mommy and I were on the terrace of our private lounge we had a talk.

"Are you enjoying the trip, baby?"

"Yes, mommy," I said bleakly. I was enjoying the trip. We were in Cancun where the water was crystal clear, perfect sunny weather, a lot of thing to get into, pampering and clothing shops. Yes even at a young age, I was a fashionista and loved entertainment.

"You don't sound like it," mommy sits up from her lounge chair and removes her shades.

"I'm ok, just thinking about daddy."

"Oh, you miss him," she puts her shades back on and returns to lying back on the chair. She looked fabulous as always in a size 4, black and white polka dot bikini. Her skin, butterscotch smooth, flawless and glowing. Her hair in her signature sleek bob hung to her chin.

"No, I don't."

"Well, what about daddy, sweetie?" She pages through her magazine.

"I know he cheated on you."

She tenses saying, "Landon, where did you get that information?"

"I overheard you arguing." I sat up and faced her.

"Overheard or eavesdropped?"

"Eavesdropped. Are you getting a divorce? I'm mad at daddy too, but I don't know if I want you to get a divorce. What are you going to do?"

"Mommy is not going to lie to you Landon. You are so mature for your age. I really don't know what I am going to do. I need to talk to your father. We need to figure things out. You know we both love you, right?"

"Do you still love him?"

She looks out to the ocean, "Unfortunately, I do."

"Why is that a bad thing?" I asked curiously.

"Landon, what I'm about to tell you I want you to take to heart. I want you to remember this talk. When you get older you will appreciate and understand what I'm about to tell you. I'm telling you this because I love you. I don't want you to ever be embarrassed or look like a fool."

"Ok, mommy."

"I'm going to be very blunt and honest. Like I said before, you are very mature."

I nod.

"Don't marry for love, marry for money. A man will say he loves you, but eventually he gives into temptation. You have two options. You can leave and search for a new man, but in the end he will cheat too and you will end up on this never ending cycle. Or, you can marry well and do you. Never, I repeat, never settle for just anybody. He must be financially SET so you can pamper yourself with I'm sorry gifts." She pauses and I process the information. "Being with a man who lies and can't offer you anything but struggle and excuses will only make life harder. Being broke and struggling with a man that cheats, the benefits are zero. I'm not saying it's easy, but you mustn't fall for love."

"So you regret being in love with daddy?"

"No, because I wouldn't have you. I just wished I used my head more than my heart. But that comes from my childhood. I was looking for love. The things I'm telling you I did not know. No one took the time out to tell me about anything. I learned from observation and experience. I'm telling you this because I don't want you to end up broken. Do you understand, honey?"

"Yes."

"Don't worry. I will continue to tell you these things. You will never be weak. My dear you are too good for that."

I smile.

She continues, "Be the conqueror not the conquered. Make men grovel at your feet, even your father. This

misfortune you witnessed, Daddy needs to pay. Make
him pay his way into your good graces and he will be
forever endowed to you. Also when dealing with men,
make sure you always have your own security, meaning
money and men."

Mommy was right. If she would have left I
would have bounced around from mommy to daddy.
Daddy no doubt would have had plenty of 'friends'.
Some would try to be my friend, using me to convince
daddy to be with them. Some would not like me, try to
ship me off when they got a chance. Life with mommy I
knew would be more stable. She would be more discreet.
I would not know her activities or "friends."

However, mommy looked at the entire picture. She
didn't want another female influencing me or thinking
they could discipline me. Plus, with mommy's crazy
work schedule it would be hard to date. Who had time
to go through the headache of weeding out the worthy
men? Again not right, but she knew daddy. He wasn't
perfect, but the good outweighed the bad. Like mommy
told me, make him pay and he did.

When we returned from our break, mommy continued giving him the cold shoulder. My conversations with
daddy remained short, the gap never closed, our bond
broken. He was very attentive and sweet. I swear he
had a gift for me and mommy every day. The situation
however bonded me with mommy I was team Jackie 100
percent. I was her best friend she shared more secrets
and taught me to pick a man like you would clothes. Go
for quality. She also told me I was quality and to never
settle. In life there is pain but always look good, fittingly
mommy and I stayed in the latest fashions.

Mommy and daddy continued to spoil me. There
were no limits for me. Vacations were always good. I
traveled to many countries and islands before the age of
18. I became accustomed to the exotic, eccentric, making
me far from average, always a lot of personality.

When it came down to it, he's greedy. My daddy
is fine, tall, smooth butter skin and has those smoky

hazel-green eyes that drove women to become stalkers. Back in his day, light skin was in. He stayed in the gym and I've seen on many occasions, despite having me in tow, how women came on to him. They would tell him they wanted to fuck him. Another bonus, him being a lawyer, everyone wanted to marry a doctor or a lawyer. Women always want successful men it didn't matter if he wore a ring or not. Just the idea of being with a man of power does something to a gal. Daddy's alluring appeal, only doing the finer things in life, didn't help. Daddy had a Mercedes before they were so accessible. He had a Mercedes when all parts were made in Germany and were special ordered. For him, women were like a new toy and after the buzz he was done. I knew with mommy that there was a difference. I do believe he loves mommy. Their arguments notorious, but the makeup sex legendary. It wasn't right, but it was all that I knew as I grew, observed and had heartache of my own.

Just as mommy said, over the years I would understand and agree. My mentality changed, especially after Jason.

2

Mr. Man

Jason Davis was this star high school football player. It's always been sports for me. Maybe daddy turned me off of white collar men I rebelled at anything similar to him. I know sports are far worse, but the money was so much better. The key is security. Back to Jason, he attended Eastland Academy, the all boy private school across the street. My father insisted I attend St. Francis, the all-girl school. I'd been in attendance since I was 7, and at the age of 15, I had enough.

A lot of people couldn't take my strong personality. While I had some friends, I wouldn't call any close friends. I did speak to all. Although some things I admit should have been left unsaid. My parents were called to the school many times due to my verbal confrontations. Each time I pointed out to my parents their profession and home environment made me naturally argumentative and I was used to getting my point across.

One person I had constant issues with was Nina Tisdale. She was a snobby, brunette, long-haired, stuck-up bitch with a big mouth and pale skin. We never got along, always had some competition going on and we both liked Jason. Nina's problem was she thought she could talk to anyone any kind of way and we were supposed to bow down to her because her parents were in the entertainment business. It was true that she got into the latest concerts, had plenty of friends but they only wanted to reap benefits. I was not a groupie.

One day during the first week of school during study period, which was in the co-ed library that joined both schools Jason approaches. Jason was a cutie. He reminds me of Lance Gross.

"Hey, Landon."

"Hello."

"You look nice today?"

"I have on the same thing every other girl has on."

He laughs. "Well you stand out because you are the prettiest."

"You have perfect vision."

It was his turn to laugh.

"Since you are attracted to my beauty, are you going to just stand and admire? If so, that's fine."

"You a trip Landon."

"You seem tongue-tied. I thought you didn't have anything else to say. You look so content staring. Would you like to see my pretty smile?"

"Landon, would you like to go to the movies?"

"Only if it's a good one."

We exchange phone numbers and quickly began a little fling.

News got back to Nina that Jason and I was together. She damn near had a tantrum and started a rumor that I was a slut. She told everyone that I had sex in bathrooms, was having threesomes, sucked dick, any and everything she could think of. Now back in the early 2000's, oral sex was not acceptable and boys were anti-eating pussy. Back then, I was a good girl, still even a virgin.

Mommy made sure we had the sex talk and stressed

not giving it to anyone. I hadn't gone all the way, but two boys had given me oral pleasure. I never returned the favor. I knew the power of a woman back then. I made false promises that I'd return the favor and had an alarm or call to come signaling it was time for me to go home.

Jason and I talked for two months with a lot of shade from Nina. For the most part, I ignored her and her followers when they called me names, which irritated her. I knew I was far prettier, so when she taunted me, I would pull out a compact mirror, apply lip gloss and blow kisses to myself. My skin, a golden hue kissed sweetly by the sun. My size two, 5'7 frame, with the perkiest C-cup tities, looked good in everything. My hair, at the time, was cut short, so I could showcase my pretty hazel green eyes. Nina wasn't anything to be concerned about.

Jason and I hung out at the movies, went skating. I liked him. I definitely had strong feelings for him. I was doing stuff out of character like blushing and anticipating his call. He was the first boy I tried oral sex on. Things were going well. All of the shade Nina was throwing was getting old and people stopped paying her or me being a "hoe" any attention until late October.

Jason and I were at his house, his parents were still at work. His sister Jade, who was best friends with Nina were at cheerleading practice. I never liked Jade. Jade was phoney. If it was me, Jason, and her, we were cool and would have fun. However, when Nina came around she was a different person and along with Nina, would throw shade. Since we were alone, we figured we could get into some things. Everything was fine. Originally, I removed my panties and laid back on Jason's bed for him to pleasure me. He gave me a few licks but stopped, saying he wanted me spread out on his bed naked. I was always comfortable with my body and had done so before. Jason on the other hand just had his pants down. He wanted me to suck his dick. I told him he had to finish eating my pussy and if he did a good job I would. He did and when I was on the verge of an orgasm he stopped and tried to slide his dick in me. I quickly put a halt to that. I wiggled from him and got up from the bed. Jason was mad.

"Landon, why you keep playing these games?"

"I'm not playing games. I told you I was not having sex with you."

"I'm supposed to eat you out and that's it? I have needs too."

"Jason, I returned the favor twice, so I'm not trying to hear that."

"Well it's time we take it to the next level. We been talking for a while."

"Well I'm not feeling that right now." I took a seat on his bed,

"So I'm just supposed to keep licking your pussy until you ready?" He asked throwing his legs over the bed and standing.

"Uh, yes." I said like it was the stupidest question in the world.

He was annoyed, but I didn't care. I was mad he tried to be slick and slip his dick in me.

I was about to put my clothes on when he asked, "Well, can you suck me off?"

He walks over and puts his semi-hard dick in my face.

"I'm sorry."

"I'm sorry too because I'm not doing it. I told you to do me right. You didn't finish and you were sneaky."

"Oh, you really are being a bitch."

Before I could say or do anything I was exposed.

Nina opens the door with an entourage, "I told you she was a slut."

Then Jason hollers, "I told you I didn't want you! Stop throwin' your stank ass pussy on me. You can suck my dick again though."

"Damn, you got shitted on," one of the guys ridiculed.

I was so hurt, but tears would not fall from these eyes. I quietly put on my clothes, too hurt, embarrassed and shocked for a rebuttal. I felt like the Carrie scene in the end when everyone is laughing at her. They ridiculed me while I dressed, making comments about my body, me. I swear I saw red. I was going to get back both at those bitches.

When I finally did make it home, I let the tears fall. I had never cried over a boy before and I definitely didn't like the feeling. I wanted to tell mommy, but I was too ashamed. She constantly drilled not to trust these little boys or men. She reminded me how they talk a good game, but I had to be better, always ten steps ahead.

The incident with Jason made private school life go from bearable to miserable. The taunting was ten times worse and boys were approaching me like I was a prostitute offering money to suck their dicks. The fake friends I had acted like being around me was like having the plague. I guess guilty by association. I really didn't care because as an only child I was used to entertaining myself. There were many days I wanted to cry, but I refused to give them the satisfaction. I asked mommy if I could transfer to another school, explaining the girls were jealous. She told me females would always be jealous of me because I was gorgeous and as just wonderful. I finally did convince her I needed diversity and she agreed to the transfer as long as daddy was on board. I begged daddy to transfer me. I told him it was too many mood swings, too much estrogen. I even told him I was being bullied. He told me I was being theatrical as usual. I really was angry with him then.

I suffered through October and November, but by December, I was able to get my revenge. It was during a combined Christmas dance for both the boys and girl

private school. A few days earlier, I overheard Nina tell
Jade she was going to give Jason some. I knew they
were going to sneak off during the dance but wasn't sure
where. Now during our school functions, it was common
for us students to put vodka in the water bottles, add
Kahlua to the hot chocolate or latte; yes, we were always
buzzed. Basically, with the brain a little relaxed it made
it the perfect opportunity for a little payback. The internet making it all possible.

Nina was a creature of habit, always ordering
a white chocolate mocha from Starbucks. This day,
I ordered the same. In my cup I added OsmoPrep.
OsmoPrep tablets contain a combination of sodium bi-
phosphate and sodium phosphate it was given to patients
to clean their bowel before a colonoscopy. I put my cup
next to hers and said something to irritate her.

"That dress doesn't look good on you. That black
with your pale skin makes you look like a vampire."
Which I really wasn't lying about. It wasn't cute at all.

"Like I would take fashion tips from a slut."

I grabbed her cup and shrugged my shoulders,
"Alright, Lady Elvira."

"Bitch," she called out.

Next, I went on a hunt for Jason. I knew him well
enough to know he would have a bottle of water. He had
a few friends with him. When they saw me, they started
laughing asking can I suck them off. I ignored them.

"Hello, Jason."

He looks over my short red dress and smiles. "Hello,
Landon."

"Can I talk to you?"

"It depends. You offering a service?"

His friends laugh. I roll my eyes. "I guess you gonna
have to come and see."

He follows me to another hall in the school. He goes
to take a swig of his water and I intentionally knock it
over. "Damn, you waste my shit."

"Stop whining, I have some Vodka. I'm sure mine tastes better." I hand him the half-filled bottle that is a mixture of vodka, cranberry and Viagra. Another pill made possible by the internet.

He takes a swig. "Yeah, you're right. Yours is better."

"You should know I am better."

"Oh, you trying to get with the program."

I smile.

He takes another sip. "So are you going to give me some or what?"

"From what I hear, you and Nina have something happening tonight."

He blows out a deep breath, "Nina will be alright."

"Why don't you admit it? My pussy smells better and tastes better than hers."

He laughs and then takes a sip.

"Oh, you trying to say I'm lying."

"Nah."

"I know it does. Too bad you clowned me that day."

He finishes the vodka bottle.

"You back on that? I was mad. You were clowning me."

"No, I wasn't. You see my pussy was better quality and worth the wait."

"Yeah, you right. Your pussy was good. I want to slide up in it."

"Ok, I thought about it and I decided. Hell to the fucking no."

"That's alright, 'cause what you won't do, Nina will."

"But like you said, my shit is better." I grabbed his hard dick, "Look, I got you hard. Nina will never make it feel as good as I can."

"Fuck you."

"I know you want to bad, but you never will." I walk away.

Jason fell right into my trap. I went back into the hall where Nina and Jade were. I knew Jason would be looking for Nina to take care of his current arousal. Within minutes, he is in Nina's face kissing her while throwing daggers at me. It doesn't take long for Nina and Jason to disappear around the hall. Prior to me instigating attacks on Jason and Nina, I made sure all the classroom and hallway doors were locked. The only door unlocked was a closet. It was a decent size and enough room to get busy. It had a bench so the only comfortable position was cowgirl.

Jade tried to talk to me since her bestie was with Jason, but I walked off to the dance. Jade followed minutes later. I went to my locker to retrieve my camera. I quietly crept to the closet Jade and Jason were in and locked the door.

I snuck off again and got Jason's friends and told them what he was doing. Of course they wanted to be nosy. Unbeknownst to Jason and Nina, there was an echo, everything could be heard.

You could hear the slurp sounds being made as Nina was sucking his dick. Me and his friends stood back and silently laughed.

"Damn, Nina. You doin' it too rough."

"I'm sorry."

"Take it easy. Do it like you did before."

"Is that better?" she asks after a few slurps.

"No. Stand up and bend over so I can fuck you," Jason says frustrated.

"I don't feel right," Nina whines.

"That's just nerves."

"I don't know. My stomach feels funny."

"Once you feel this dick in you it will be fine."

"You're right."

"You want it rough like always."

"Yes," she moans.

"Nina, move around instead of just sitting there."

"Unh, Unh," she grunts.

"I'm going to put it in your ass."

"Ok, fuck me Jason."

"It's tight. Wiggle yo' ass, so I can slide in. It hurt?"

"It hurts, but just keep sliding in. it will feel good in a few minutes. I've done it before."

He lets out a moan.

"I told you it would feel good once it's in. Fuck me hard."

We hear a couple of loud pangs before Jason screams out in horror, "Ah, what the fuck?! Why yo' ass so slimy? What the hell is that smell?!"

"I got to go to the bathroom."

I see the door rattling, but she can't open it because I locked it

"Nasty bitch, get off of me."

"I can't stop. My stomach! Oh my God, my stomach! I can't stop shittin'!"

"Your ass stinks! I'm about to earl. Open the fucking door!"

"I can't!"

By now, his friends and I are crying laughing. Other bystanders come out to see what all of the ruckus is about. Someone has mercy and opens the door. They should have left it closed. The smell of her shit was horrendous and damn near knocked me out. Damn near, but didn't. I aim my camera snapping the Kodak moment of Nina's petrified face, Jason's horror and shit running down his legs.

She got up and slipped in her shit, given us the perfect view of Jason's rock hard dick.

Payback time, I couldn't resist taunting his ass, referring to the infamous scat-fetish pornographic film. "Damn you like that two girls and a cup shit? You ready for another round? You wanted to do your own video."

Everyone was laughing. Nina gets up, I was ready. "You a dirty hoe. You take it up the ass. I bet you like golden showers too. Damn, you stink! You need a healthier diet."

She runs off crying.

I get serious and look at Jason, "What you got to say now dirty dick motherfucker? And who pussy smells like shit now? I'd say Nina!" I taunt. "Ass man, I see. Now I see why you loved lickin' Nina's ass."

I turn to the boy who made the comment about me getting shitted on a few weeks ago, "Jason is the one who got shitted on."

Of course there was a school investigation after that fiasco. A week later when Nina and Jason were better, we all along with our parents, were called into the principal's office. No one had proof that I set things up, but I was seen with a bottle containing questionable substances. Some student saw me knock over Jason's vodka, give him more, and told after the fact. I was reprimanded. Nina and Jason of course, had all type of violations for having sex in school, drinking, and more, but I zoned out for most of the lecture. For my mischief, I was suspended for 7 days, put on academic probation and some other crap. It didn't matter, daddy would transfer me. I had enough of these bitches. If he played hardball, then I would have to hit him below the belt, and I did.

"Landon," my father gives me an evil stare.

"Yes, daddy," I sang sweetly.

"I'm not going back and forth with you. You will be returning back to private school. You are there to learn, meaning that is your priority. You will be on your best behavior. No more mishaps."

"Daddy, I told you I am not excelling emotionally or socially there. I am the victim. The girls have a problem with me because I am strong-willed."

"Landon, you are there to excel academically. This will prepare you for your adult years. This is a platform, the possibilities you have are endless. You will be well-rounded and it will benefit you."

"Daddy, I've been there since I was seven. That school is not the right fit for me. It's time for me to move on. I need to be exposed to more culture. When I am an adult and I am in the real world I need to communicate with people with different social backgrounds."

My father shakes his head. "Landon, what career have you chosen for your future?"

Uhh, I really hadn't thought about it much, I lied. "A lawyer, daddy, like you and mommy."

He wasn't buying it. "Why do you want to be a lawyer, Landon?"

"Daddy, I don't want to go there anymore," I folded my arms across my chest and took a seat in the chair.

"Landon, you are going back there."

"You act as if my zoned school is horrible. It was ranked in the top 10 public schools in the country."

"Very good Landon, you did your research. The answer, however, is still no."

"Daddy, you're not being fair," I pouted.

"Landon, you're too old for tantrums."

He pissed me off with that comment. He was about to get it. "Daddy, you taught me there is always ways to negotiate. The key is making sure you are the negotiator and of course hold all the evidence.

"I taught you?"

"Yes, so what is it going to be?"

"Public school is not what's best for you."

"Neither is cheating on mommy. Do you realize how much damage you've done to my young impressionable mind? Do you realize from your behavior, I will have a hard time or may never trust a man?"

"You shouldn't trust them."

"I don't and I thank you daddy for making sure I never will."

I played hooky from school last week with CJ. CJ was a senior at Eastern Academy. We'd played hooky usually twice a month, sometimes more. I would miss my hooky days with him. He was a big gay teddy bear. He loved my style and loved to hang out with me for fashion tips and acceptance He too was ridiculed for his sexual preference, me because of Jason. Last week, we went to the mall which is across the street from a hotel and lo and behold, there he was…my daddy. You know the rest. He really was a sloppy, pathetic cheater.

"Landon."

"Daddy, save it."

"Landon."

"Daddy, really, the less you say the better. Don't insult me with lying. I know what I saw. I know it wasn't the first time and I'm sure it won't be the last."

"Landon you will not talk to me any type of way. I am your father," he says in his courtroom voice.

I give him my sweet innocent little girl voice. "I am your daughter. It hurts me to see mommy. She loves you. Do you know how many tears she cried because of you? How many tears I cried? I am now forced to live your lie and pretend I never saw you with another woman."

He takes a breath.

"Daddy."

"Yes, Landon," he says painfully.

"What day will I be transferred? Monday works for me."

"Landon you will not manipulate me."

"I'm not. I'm negotiating. Now daddy do you really want me to go to mommy. Do you remember when I was 12, how mommy and I took a vacation because you cheated. Yes, I knew. It didn't go over well. I'm older now. I don't adore you like before. I see you for what you are."

"Landon, I'm sorry you witnessed that."

"I'm sorry too, daddy."

"Landon, I will transfer you on Monday."

"Thank you, daddy. I'm going to go check on mommy."

Eventually I did confess to mommy the origin of the private school fiasco. Mommy wasn't as disappointed as I thought she would be.

She actually was sympathetic. She told me we all had setbacks just don't stay back; rise above, be even better and more cautious the next time. She was happy I stood my ground and didn't lose my virginity. She did make an appointment to get me on birth control just in case I felt the urge. But she stressed not to rush because once I go down that road that will open up a whole new set of emotions. She said if I thought I made a bad decision before, sex would make me even more emotional. She pleaded and I waited. She advised me that when I do give someone that gift make sure they deserve it. She stressed again that I was the best and shouldn't give or deal with anyone that's not on my level. The person I give my gift to should make me top priority, be driven and worthy. My private school and daddy experience taught me how to get what I wanted on my terms; taught me how to use power.

3

Cherish The Day

"Land, oh my god, Land! Diva if anyone can pull through this, it's you. Fight, I know it's hard, but you have to fight. You got so much to fight for. Stay strong, please diva."

It was Yas.

Forcing daddy's hand to transfer me to public school was the smartest thing I did. It was there I met Yasmin. Her friendship, her influence, impacted me on so many levels. Yasmin and I were ten months apart, but in the same grade. We bonded from the beginning, later we would understand that bond. I wanted to smile, hug my sister. We were finally making up, mending our broken relationship. It can't end like this. I need to talk to her again tell her I love her and appreciate how she never let me down. The last year without her has been hell. Damn, I wish I could spend a day with my friend like the old days. It was true when they said you don't miss what you got till it's gone. We had so much more to say, so much more to do. Although she is stubborn, drove me crazy with her lectures, and her too reserved demeanor, she was always loyal. She never lied to me, put pressure on me. While she definitely never agreed with my antics, she never judged or ridiculed. She always accepted me as I am. She told me more than once how she admired my tenacity and wit. I always admired her for her strength. Whether it was her mother treatment towards me, break-ups, losses, she was strong and would be my shoulder. I honestly hated that I was not that person for her and I was the one who hurt her the most. Yes, I was confident, independent, just like mommy wanted. Yasmin, however was my best friend, sister, road dog, the one I didn't have to put up a façade for. I could reveal my weaknesses to her.

Yasmin was quiet, but for some reason I was drawn to her. She was plain, no flash, but I knew she was pretty. She had a sad aura about her. It was crazy because normally I wouldn't care, but it was like she was crying out for my assistance. She started out as a project but I grew attached to her naivety and genuineness. She quickly became the only person I could trust. She wasn't my friend because I had money or wanted to be in the popular crowd. In fact, she hated attention. With a little persuasion, I could get her to do things. But I knew from the beginning she would always have my back.

"Land, remember when we were in college and you got me drunk to loosen me up some? Remember how we went to the karaoke bar. It was then, you first found out I could sing. You knew I needed extra cash so you found the karaoke bars that paid cash for first place." Yasmin begins to cry. After a moment she continues. "You choreographed a rendition of En Vogue version of *"Giving Him Something He Can Feel"*. You made sure to get me drunk before every performance, but we won. You made me keep all the money. Thank you again." I hear her take in more breaths. "Remember the night we met the guys who went to Hampton? Now that was an adventure. We ended up in Atlantic City. I know I fussed, but I will now admit that was the best college experience I had. You were always the life of the party. Everybody loved hanging with you. Always the center of attention. I wish I could have been more like you. I loved that. I wish I was more comfortable in my skin. Then again

there may have been some arrests for indecent proposal."
She laughed. "We had so much fun. What about our trips
to New York, like the city, we never slept. Boy, do we
have some stories."

"Damn, Landon. I need you to get up and start
giving me some demands. Go ahead so I can do what I
always do, ignore you." Kevin says, voice cracking.

Kevin worked at my parents' law firm. Kevin was
only three years older than Yassy and I. My parents
respected Kevin's work ethic and became like the son
daddy never had, which was okay with me. I was team
Jacqueline Taylor. Kevin was a nice guy who I believe
daddy secretly tried to match me up with. Kevin was
chocolate, the way I like, very sexy, six-pack abs, tall,
model looks, but he was too boring and I knew he was
smitten with Yasmin. In the beginning, I thought they
would make a boring, but cute couple. Yasmin never
liked him in that way, like me, she considered him an
older brother. Kevin, I think, finally got the picture.
Kevin was my big brother in every sense. He intervened
on several occasions when I needed legal counsel. He
drew up contracts for me at the last minute, defended
me, and best of all, he never told my parents about any
of my legal trouble.

"I can't believe this happened," Kevin says.

"I know. I just left her a few hours ago. I could tell
she was stressed, but I figured it was everything going on
with us. I should have known it was something more."

I hear Yasmin sniffle.

"Yas, you couldn't have known this would happen."

"Kevin, it was surreal. Landon spoke to me like
she knew something would happen. She told me time
is precious. Something you cannot get back. Time was
something you should cherish. She also told me don't let
pride get in the way of me being happy. Remember what
and who makes me happy."

"Landon said that?"

"I know."

If I could I would have burst with laughter. That really didn't sound like me. If only they knew all the things that transpired, all the things I had gotten into. Maybe then, they could understand. I feel so tired. I want to sleep, but I'm scared if I let go, I will be letting go of life. I'm not ready. I don't want to leave my brother and sister, but I need some rest.

I hear Yasmin vaguely speak she sounds far away, "Land I know we've had a hard year. It's been rough, but I love you. When you came in my life I was able to live, enjoy it. You made me get out of my shell. You helped build me. You are my crazy diva. I've been so lost I need you, please don't leave me. I know I said some things, but diva you deserved it."

She was so right. I deserved what she said and more.

"Diva you can't leave me like this. Wake up, I know you got a rebuttal. Diva come back, I need you. Tell you what, I'll let you style me for a few months, even cut my hair."

Oh how I wish I could have jumped and spoke on that one. I've been trying to get Yassy to show off her curvy body for years. She was always self-conscious of her 10-12 size. Yasmin didn't realize her 5'11 frame, and size 10/12 looked damned good. Her thick hair that hung to the middle of her back she used to hide her pretty face. Our faces held a lot of similarities, our hazel-green eyes hypnotizing showstoppers complementing our golden honey complexion. Yes, the things I wish I could do.

"Come on beautiful. We will come back tomorrow." Says Braxton.

Oh, here we go. Braxton, Yasmin's husband, the father of my son, as usual, his jealous controlling ass is interfering with my Yassy time. He irked the hell out of me. If I opened my eyes, I would see Yasmin's back pressed tightly against his chest. Both of his arms wrapped around her so she can't move. I'm sure his lips are pressed right on her cheek. Sickening, right? Oh how I wish I could throw a shoe and knock him out.

"I'm not ready yet, she might wake up."

"If she does, I will bring you back."

I wanted to scream leave my girl alone, but I couldn't. She told you she wanted to stay with me and I don't want her to go. I can't stand him.

He continues, "Yasmin, I know it's hard, but you need to lie down, eat something, and we need to check in on the kids."

I hate when he's right. Yassy, go. I aint going yet or at least I hope not.

"Yasmin if anything changes, I will let you know."

"Thanks Kevin, we appreciate that." Braxton quickly speaks up.

Oh, that was funny. Braxton is still jealous of Kevin. I know Braxton really had her hemmed up in that bear hug. I wonder if she will give Kevin a hug. Definitely no good being a fly on the wall when you can't see. Woo, I'm so tired. I need my rest. Ok, I'm going to rest. Try to wrap my brain around when, how, why this disaster all got started. Try to figure out if I can't get myself out of this grave I dug. Where do I begin? I guess then I should begin with Eric since he is a major factor.

4

Pardon Me

I was sitting in the service area at the local Mercedes dealer when he walked in. The temperature was a chilling 15 degrees, but the way he walked, his wardrobe, dark shades, hat, said the thermometer was a liar. His aura yelled it was a 100 degrees but he looked cool, a mere 70 degrees. I normally don't stare, but I liked what I saw. Smooth dark chocolate on a 6'8 slender frame.

He sees me eyeing him. I make it no secret.

"Hello," he says in a deep baritone.

"Hello handsome."

He smiles, I get to see his teeth are straight and white. Good. Nothing is more of a turn-off than seeing someone who's obviously well off, can afford dental care, but don't invest.

"So do you make it a habit of flirting with men in the dealership?"

"Who said I was flirting. I was just giving you a compliment. I'm going to give you another. Nice teeth. What do those eyes look like?"

"That's not flirting?"

"No, if I were, I would be more direct. "You would know the difference between the two."

Just then the service representative comes out, "Ms. Taylor, your car is ready."

"Thank you, I'll be right over."

I walked over to tall, dark, and sexy. "My name is Landon. You are just what I needed to warm me up this cold morning. I'd like to continue this discussion," I hand him my business card.

"You're into real estate?"

"You look surprised."

"You don't look…"

"Speechless already?"

He laughs.

"Yes, I am into real estate. I have my own office. I am very skilled and have quite an impressive client list to be twenty-two. As much as I would like to tell you more, I have a meeting."

"Nice to meet you Landon."

"It was definitely a pleasure. It would be even nicer if you give me your name."

"Eric."

"Well Eric, perhaps I'll talk to you later."

Eric didn't call me that day. Three weeks later, still nothing. I had forgotten about him until one day he shows up in my office, flowers in hand, just as sexy as before.

"Hello Landon."

"So you did remember me. I was beginning to think I didn't make a good impression.

"No, you were impressive."

"I'm glad to hear that."

"Landon, I'd like to take you up on your offer. Find out the difference between the two."

"My schedule is open. You pick a day and a time."

"The day I pick is today. The time is now. I will require your whole day."

"Very wise man. Carpe Diem."

Eric and I hit it off from the start. Definitely a gentle soul gentleman and that scared the hell out of me. He made it very hard enlisting me as his real estate agent. I found out he played for the Washington Wizard's, had excellent credit 800 plus credit score, yes exceptional and eight-figures in the bank. Mommy warned me about men like this. Daddy showed me. Double whammy I would not be the triple. On most occasions when we were together I came very close to having sex with him. I wasn't prepared for the emotions that came along with Eric. I used Will to distract me from Eric.

Will played cornerback for the Baltimore Ravens. I really didn't like him. His attitude was the worst, but I kept him around because he was shallow. He was a constant reminder of why I had to stay focused, not fall for the crap these men are constantly talking. I knew his game, he was a lot of fun, but I knew he was short-term. He used me as a trophy on his arm and in return, lavished me with gifts and money. So yes, we used each other.

5

Girl

At 22 I was not a virgin. I actually managed to hold onto my virginity until I was 18. I gave my jewel to Chris. Chris at first was really sweet, but they all are. He told me how pretty I was bought me things truly pampered me. Even minor details were covered such as car mainte- nance, soup when I was sick and his tongue was the best. He had me seeing stars and after three months, he earned it. Mommy said sex would bring on a new set of emo- tions, for Chris, it most certainly did. He became posses- sive, monitoring my calls, knew my schedule better than me. He thought he could pick out my friends, really iso- late me. Anytime you had a problem with quiet, reserved Yasmin who stayed in the shadows, you had a problem. He was obsessed. Getting rid of him was havoc; he was literally stalking me. I broke it off and the asshole hit me. Fortunately, due to my outgoing personality, I had a lot of male friends. They ran his ass off the campus. Years later, however, he resurfaced, still obsessed. I had to enlist my new adopted brother Kevin to file papers and pay him a visit. Last I heard, he found someone to marry him, poor soul whoever she is.

Now you can see why I have to screen these men, they will literally snap. If they are that attentive and loving on you, watch out. I know not all men are like that but they have issues with being possessive, a cheat-er, a liar, or weak-minded. I had no desire for any of the above. So to settle down with these men and all the different personas? Hell no! My personality was enough. Hence the reason why I fuck with a certain type. I know what I got. I love surprises, but not when it comes to crazy, possessed, or pussy whipped men.

Like now, I'm supposed to be hanging with my best friend in the world and she all gaga on this fool Braxton. He's cute, I give him that, but I love dark chocolate. I don't discriminate, I date them all, but something about smooth dark chocolate skin just melts in your mouth. Braxton has her open for foolery. His whole swagger and attitude already told me what she was dealing with. On their first date, the fool couldn't even show up on time. Then he takes her to Dave and Buster's, I mean, he liter-ally told your ass right there he was about game. Another thing, the possessive thing, he either got a hand problem, meaning physical abuse or guilty conscience because like I said, he runnin' game. It's definitely the latter, he's fucking other chicks. Yasmin's aloofness was definitely killing my vibe.

"Yassy, enough."

"Huh."

"You killing me taking about Bastard."

"Braxton," she said, sounding offended.

I laugh. "Well, you knew who I was talking about."

"I'm sorry Landon that I didn't allow you an hour to talk about yourself and your men," she says sarcastically.

I give it right back to her, "Not a problem, darling. I know I'm just lovely aren't I. My men just love me. So many of them want my time, my affection, but I don't have the energy. It's lovely having options and so many varieties. You must try it."

We both bust out laughing.

"Land, I'm sorry was I that bad?"

"You're getting that bad. Don't drag him to the chapel."

"I'm not trying to do that. I'm not ready for that. He has issues."

"Do tell."

"You know. His jealousy."

"Yassy, think. Be honest. You don't think he would hit you do you?"

"Oh no!"

"Are you sure?"

"Yes. He's like you, spoiled. Just use to getting his way, has a tantrum when you think someone is trying to steal your friend."

"I am not like that."

"My bestest friend in the world, yes, you are."

I pout.

"You know it's the truth. Get over yourself."

I stick out my tongue.

She rolls her eyes.

"I still think you and Kevin would be the cutest couple."

"I know you're wrong."

"What's wrong with Kevin? He loves himself some Yassy."

"Landon, please. You and I both know you can only deal with Kevin in spurts. He is so long-winded."

She was right, but I wouldn't admit it. "He is not. Kevin is sexy and he will give you the world. And I'm sure he can work the tongue. When he starts talking too much, tell him licky, licky."

She laughs. "I'll pass."

"Kevin is the best choice."

Shaking her head, she asks, "Well diva, how are your men, Eric and Will, right?"

"Time for a change, Will is annoying. Eric is too clingy."

"Well, I know their replacements with have to be on their A game."

"Only way I deal with them. I deserve the best because I am the best."

"I hear you, Diva."

"Yassy, you deserve the best also. I will be watching Bastard."

She laughs. "I know you will. I know you got my back and I love you for it."

"Love you too, Yassy."

Spending time with my Yassy as always was wonderful. The whole day we pampered ourselves, spa, hair, manicure, pedicure, dinner, more girl talk. As a pretty girl, I've had my share of jealousy along with cattiness. A lot of drama, some of which I caused, because I love the attention from men, but I loved having a genuine friendship more.

6

So Over You

"Say my name, say my name," he grunted.

I focus on blocking him out, imagining I was getting pounded by a dark chocolate specimen. More than anything else, I'm enjoying his plush bed covered in the finest silk sheets.

"Say my name, say my name." Missionary style, he thinks he is working it. It ain't bad, but it ain't great either. "Say my name, say my name," he continues.

I roll my eyes, this fool sounds just like a queen Beyoncé. He don't realize I aint the one.

"Let me ride the dick," I moan.

"Say my name."

"I want to ride the dick."

"Landon, say my name and then you can ride this dick."

I close my eyes imagining it was not Will gliding in me, imagined it was Mr. Sexy dark chocolate sucking my nipples."

"Damn baby, this dick good ain't it. You so wet."

"Lick my pussy," I order.

I needed to climax so I could leave. Will was really boring me.

"You can't handle this dick."

This time I would say his name. "Will mmmm, lick my pussy, baby. I can't take this dick."

It took a lot of restraint not to laugh at his arrogant ass. The way his face lit up reminded me of cartoon character.

"Will lick it, baby, let's see how many licks its takes to get Landon to scream.

"Damn, Landon, you so wet. I'm about to bust this nut," he says before he starts shaking like he is seizing.

I only give him a minute before I demand, "Lick it!"

He does, slithering his tongue down my body on his pursuit to my jewel. Slow teasing licks he takes that were aggravating me more than pleasuring me. Nothing I hated more than telling a man how to please a woman. His days were so numbered. Concentrate on your dark chocolate treat that has a clear schedule next week. Yes, sexy, his ass would do this thing right without any instruction or guidance. Just remembering the last time we were together my body started to shudder. His tongue sucked my sweet nectar like a cherry candy ball. Umm yes, the sweet memory.

"Ahh, damn, shiiit oh shiit!" I finally scream out. I need to call my dark chocolate sexy piece ASAP.

"I handled it didn't I, Landon?" Will rolls on his back.

Let me think sexy was in Sacramento, which is three hours behind. Its 11:30 now. So I need to shower, check ESPN to see if his team won and make my call. Ok, enough lying around, time to go. I sit up, swinging my legs around the side of the bed.

"I did my thing. You like that didn't you?"

I give the fakest smile I could muster.

Will grabs me by the waist, pulling me back on the bed. The condom he had on now removed, dick semi-hard. "Mr. Perfect wants a kiss."

I remove myself from his embrace and blow his dick a kiss.

"Oh, you want to play?"

"No, I want to go. I'll talk to you later."

I stood up, grabbing my clothes.

"You serious?"

I don't hide the annoyance on my face. Let's see, I'm standing with clothes in my hand, heading to the shower.

"We're not finished."

"You said you bust a nut. I had a moment. We're equal."

"You didn't suck Mr. Perfect."

"What gave you the impression that I was?"

"Last time my face was in between your pussy, giving you orgasm after orgasm you said you would take care of me next time."

This is the bullshit I hated with him, over inflating his abilities. Now I have to set the fool straight. "First of all, I have never had multiple orgasms with you. Sec-"

He cuts me off, "You a damn liar."

As much as I wanted to argue and prove he was delusional, I had a phone call to make. I went to my second point. "You're right, I did tell you I would take care of you. And I did, didn't your ass just seize in my pussy."

"Landon, see, you know you wrong."

He about to start whining like a baby, I can feel it. "Will, did I ever tell you I would suck your dick? Have I ever sucked your dick?"

"No and that's the damn problem. You always want me to eat your pussy, but can't return the favor. You're selfish."

Is he got damn serious? "Will, I ask you and you do. Do I put a gun up to your head and force you? No, I don't. You asked me, I said no several times and I never actually said I would suck your dick. There are no games or miscommunication. You were choosing to hear what you wanted to. Can we agree?"

"No, it should be a given."

"Says who?"

"You ain't playing fair."

"Will that just ain't my thing." I lied.

"So you not gonna suck my dick?"

"No."

"Well, I ain't gonna lick, eat or taste your pussy no more."

"So you're going to punish yourself. You know it tastes good. That's why you don't have a problem going there. It's good and you know it." I smile.

He doesn't say anything.

"You know you like to lick in between my legs. You like the filling. I'm so sweet, taste so good." I sing.

He blushes.

"Sorry Will, maybe if our relationship was a little more serious I would try. You know I love to please. Even though it's not my thing, for you, if we were serious, I would try. Do you want to talk about taking it to the next level?"

The expression on his face was priceless.

"Next level? Wwwhat you mean?" he stutters.

"You know what I mean. Move in together. Go house shopping. Meet the family."

"Oh, I uh, I uh. You ready for that?"

Hell no, I wanted to scream, but had to get this fool under control. Having a damn tantrum because I didn't suck his dick, he left me no choice but to be dramatic.

"I would love to meet your family, move in together. In six months we could be engaged, have a wedding next year, have a kid or three. I always wanted at least three kids. You know it was lonely being an only child."

He looks horrified.

"Will would you want a Will Jr.? Wow, who thought this conversation would end up here." I beam.

I could tell that he was struggling trying to come up with a way to get out of this. His ass won't be asking me to suck his damn dick again. His ass wanted to settle down as much as my ass did, not at mutherfuckin' all. That's why I fucked with him. He was too arrogant to be tied down or claim any one woman. He loved different women. He wasn't about trying to sneak around and jeopardize his money with alimony or child support. He has plenty of groupies who are willing to suck his dick at the snap of his fingers. He needs to get a grip.

"Landon."

I save him. "Will, listen to me running off. I think we need to slow down. We're both young in our prime. Let's not move too fast. Let's keep our relationship as it is for now. I need to focus on my business. You need to focus on your game." I walk into his moderate bathroom to shower. When I come out fully dressed, he looks just as dumbfounded as before.

"We good, Landon."

"Why wouldn't we be? Come lock up after me."

He follows, before I leave out the door, I give him a kiss on the cheek. "Later, Will."

I need some intellectual stimulation after that wack ass sex. What a damn waste. Sex with Will wasn't always a chore. Actually it was good because he is very spontaneous, he was game anytime, anyplace. Everything changed when Sexy dark chocolate came into my life. Sexy has yet to penetrate me with his tool but his tongue had and I haven't been right ever since. I wanted to take it there, but I had to get my emotions under control. I could not fall for him. I did however return the favor. Yes, which like I told Will I was not into, but with him I had a strong desire too. When I did get his tool in my mouth, like I said it turned me on even more. Like him it was extra-long, slim and dark. I had no problem relaxing my throat muscle sucking in all of him. Even surprised myself that I didn't gag when he released his pleasure in my mouth. Instead, I drank him up, enjoying his sweetness. *Get a grip Landon.* I knew it would only be a matter of time before I gave into temptation. No I was going to give in. I had to see if he could deliver. Hardest thing will be me holding out for a few weeks.

Contrary to popular belief, I am not a hoe, loose, whore or whatever term people assume I am. I do accept the title of flirt. I admit I have an abundance of male associates, but I haven't fucked a fourth of them. I've given oral sex to an eighth of them. Now when it came to them pleasing me, over half of them have. I know that was an extremely dangerous game because not many men (like Will showed earlier) will do you and they get nothing. I have been very fortunate to only have a handful of incidents, my hand game helped a lot. Oh yes, I kept an arousal stimulant that I would use when I gave a man a hand job. Most came quick within two minutes and would be embarrassed. Then, they would either leave things as they were, scared of a repeat experience or want to fuck to prove they could handle their shit. I usually challenged them to make me come in two minutes with the tongue first. If not, it was a "no go" if so, we could talk. Like I said, I'd been lucky with very few incidents.

I know it's a terrible thing to do but I love oral stimulation. I love to see a man between my legs. I love to feel his tongue on my clit. Mommy taught me not to be 'loose,' but I've always had a sexual appetite. Which I guess I can say I inherited from Daddy, he stayed in shit which I still caught him in. Well, it's been a few years, for mommy's sake, I hope he had enough. I have listened to Mommy. I only deal sexually with two men at a time.

I wait 3-4 weeks between sex with one. I only fuck guys that I see being with for six months, so technically 2 guys a year. I did not spread my jewel everywhere. Yes, quite a few had a taste but not everyone has had the treat. I was working on that. Before you get the wrong idea, you had to meet my requirements. One being whoever I engaged with had a substantial bank account.

All this sex talk had me in need. As soon as I walked into my condo, I turned to ESPN to wait for the game scores. I ran bath water while I waited for the game update. I slid into my Jacuzzi hot bubble bath, added coconut milk, honey, and ginger.

I dialed the number and when sexy answered, my jewel thumped.

"Hey handsome, I been thinking of you."

"You have."

"I sure have. Great game by the way."

"I could see some of it. I was working on a contract."

"You stay on the grind. I like how you handle your business."

I blush, glad he wasn't there to see my face. "Well, there's a lot I like about you. When you come back to town, you should let me take you out."

"I can't resist that offer."

"Well darling, you won't be disappointed."

Now You Know Better

"So, that don't mean you gotta be a bitch."

"Excuse you."

I was sitting in the lounge area of Posh lounge having a drink with Marcus Anderson a sports analyst for ESPN. I met him when he enlisted my services to buy a house. I know, another damn client. The rule is never mix business with pleasure, in my case, I disagree. I loved my career it allowed me to screen potential suitors. When I showed a man a house he had to get pre-qualified. Some bought out in cash, but thanks to Uncle Sam anything over $10,000 had to be reported. In that case, social security had to be provided in addition to all those other important questions such as criminal background. A red flag that I encountered on several occasions were clients using their "MAMA" name. That meant bad credit, had a main chick, or was ducking something.

Marcus had just closed on a property in Georgetown right in the DC metropolitan area. His credit and bank account exceeded my qualifications. He paid $1.7 million for the property, so I had a very nice commission. He wanted to take me out to celebrate. Appearance wise, he was average. I know because of his position he had to be professional at all times to avoid moral conduct breach of contracts, but he did nothing for me. I was going to use him as a replacement for Will, but I need some attraction.

"You heard me, our business is settled. I'm ready for the personal relationship. Are we going to fuck tonight?" Marcus rubs my leg.

"No, Marcus. That was never a part of the agreement. More importantly it's not going to happen."

"You just got a nice commission off of me. You owe me."

"I don't owe you shit. I earned my check."

"Your ass is a hoe, don't act like you don't fuck for money or should I say anyone whose bank account has eight figures."

"I don't fuck anyone, just like I'm not fucking you. I have my own money, thank you for adding to my account. With your eight figures you need to invest in some dental work. No one will touch any lips of mine that has see-saw teeth. Really, you got the top done it just makes sense to do the bottom. You are in no way qualified to even smell my jewel or take a look. I deal with quality. Just like your career in the field was short lived, so are you. I heard the rumors and have seen the little package you're working with courtesy of diary of a street king." I held up my pinky finger.

"Fuck you bitch."

"Not going to happen. Like you said, our business is done. Poof, be gone."

"I'm going to get your ass back."

"You that pressed for pussy? Really?" I shake my head.

I could tell he wanted to slap me, but he knew better in a busy establishment. He does what's best and leaves, but not before saying, "It ain't over."

This crap right here. Damn, looks like I'll be

keeping Will around longer than I planned. I really have been slipping, I totally missed the bottom teeth looking like a jig saw. He is on TV. It's obvious you should have your shit corrected. Glad he showed his ass now. I would have been pissed if I gave him the time, especially since he was average looking like Theo Huxtable.

Deep in thought regarding my next move, I didn't see the sexiness coming towards me until he handed me a drink. "You look like you need this."

"Hey, handsome." I attempted to say it coolly, but he had me blushing. I couldn't control my smile or the excitement in my voice.

He takes a seat next to me, "You look like you're having a rough day." He looks genuinely concerned and I hated the way I was feeling.

"I had a difficult client. Fortunately, our business is done."

"Glad to hear that. I don't like seeing that pretty face of yours frowned up."

I smile. "Well, now that you're here, it is so much better."

He smiles. Those dimples again, they're willing me in. I will resist temptation. "So does this mean you have time for me? We can look for property and become better acquainted."

"Oh, definitely, I'm looking forward to learning about the magnificent Eric Ayres."

"Likewise."

I take a sip of my drink. "You know me well, Grand Marnier and Ginger."

"Tastes just like you."

Damn, I couldn't even hide the tremor in my body, my eyes from closing, or biting the bottom of my lip.

He grabs my chin and proceeds to give me the most sensual kiss I've ever experienced. His tongue has no boundaries, teasing me, exciting me all at once. He sucks my tongue, my lips my tongue again.

I'm wet, feeling the liquid run between my thighs, I jump. Realizing I spilled my cold ass drink in my lap, I cover my face, embarrassed. Too shocked to speak, literally tongue tied. I guess there's a first time for everything.

"Damn sweetheart, if we weren't here I would spread your legs and drink that up and more."

Another tremor. He quickly goes to retrieve some napkins.

I get up what I could. So glad I chose the black romper. I excuse myself to the bathroom, the damage was minimal. Standing in front of the hand dryer erased any damage.

On my way back to Eric, I see an image I wish I hadn't. The DJ was playing Sean Paul "Give it to Me". The drums from the song had the crowd grinding, feeling the beat, but not as much as Melania. She's a Puerto Rican hoe with 36-24-38 measurements. No doubt the 38 bottom was surgically enhanced. She wore her black satin hair long, past her shoulders. Her skin was a chestnut hue, round face, doe eyes with Bambi eyelashes. I give it to her, her make-up was always on point. She was pretty. I just couldn't stand her or her snotty friends.

She and I have had this rivalry since I dated Paul. So glad we never had any type of intercourse. He was a heavyweight boxer who had just won a $150 million dollar fight. I know groupies have no rules or boundaries, but I had a talk with her. She was first in the wrong for openly flirting with him in my face, winking, walking pass him bumping into him, always in his face, making sure he saw her body. I pulled her up like a lady and tried to talk to her. I explained to her the importance of respect, even told her what happened when I wasn't around I had no control over. But, I stressed that in my face, she will show some respect.

Imagine my disgust when I saw this hooker's legs spread open with his head in between at a damn party in the middle of the floor in front of 100 people. I swear the bitch smirked. One thing I didn't do was fight over dick. With these athletes it's the norm for hookers like Melania to throw the pussy in their face. Nine out of 10 times they take it. She wasn't the first, wouldn't be the last. So why fight? Fighting just inflated their egos more. I knew Paul had no loyalty to me, but it's about principle. To add more insult, she not only fucked him, she convinced him to go with another realtor. That hoe messed up my money so she will always be on my list. Rumor had it, he gave her ass syphilis. I couldn't have been happier.

Looking at her, I knew nothing had changed. The way she was grinding her body on him, girlfriend, wife, she could care less. Not her problem or concern. Looking at her dance partner, the way he hugged her body, rubbing his hands up and down her body, he enjoyed every grind. She enjoyed every touch and soon they would be taking their dance behind closed doors.

Pure disgust resided on my face. No doubt she was a tramp, slut, but her partner.

This punk got my girl sprung, thinking he is the best thing since sliced bread. I told Yassy about falling in love. Her sprung ass will justify him in some bitch face if I tell her. He got her naïve ass gone. She will say something dumb like, it's just a dance, not realizing what a whore Melania is. I wouldn't tell her because she would swear I was exaggerating because I was jealous she hasn't' been hanging with me as much. I could, however, spook his wannabe pimp ass.

I walk over to Braxton, "Braxton, I thought that was you." I smile, never acknowledging Melania.

He looks at me and instantly I see that, "Oh shit!" look.

Melania, Ms. Desperate bitch, assumed I was trying to get Braxton from her. Just like my high school nemesis, Nina, that bitch was sneaky. "He's occupied." I couldn't resist the challenge. Yes, I wanted him but not for the reasons she thought.

"Was I talking to you or do I look like I even care? I'm sure Braxton wants to talk to me."

He whispered something in Melania's ear. I knew she was pissed by the glare she gave him, but she ultimately walked away. I did a "shoo" movement with my hand and added a smirk.

She stormed off. I wasted no time getting to the point. I focused on Braxton.

"So Yassy know about that hoe?"

"That's none of your business."

"Yasmin is my business."

"Look Landon, I'm not doing this tit for tat shit with you. Again, what Yasmin and I have going on is our business."

"Again, I think she should know you fuckin' a hooker."

"You can stir some shit up if you want, but Yasmin and I have an understanding," he winks.

Oh this cocky motherfucker. "Is that what you think?"

"No, that's what I know."

"Understanding? Really? So, if I decide to hook Yasmin up with a sexy ass man who looks better and whose pockets are long it won't interfere with your relationship? Your open door understanding applies both ways."

"You can try, but Yasmin is content."

"Oh so you think you the only one who can make Yassy have an orgasm? I will tell you plenty of ballers have inquired about my friend. I know she can do better and, quite frankly, I think she should, especially since you fuckin' that hoe Melania."

He laughs, "No doubt many have inquired, but I'm the only one who has the position. I'm the only one she wants. So your little threats are meaningless. Say something, see how it goes."

His arrogance irritates the hell out of me.

Before I could respond, Melania slithers her way over with her flunky Ty. Ty was her sidekick that stayed attached to her hip, lips on her ass. She must have been having separation issues. I can't stand neither one of these three lying ass, sneaky, conniving, arrogant motherfuckers. More than likely there nasty asses were on the way to do a three-way.

"I'm back," Melania announces.

"And your point?"

"You can leave." Ty speaks up.

"Damn, do you wipe her ass for her too?"

"No, I leave that for you since you're always in my shit."Melania comments.

Braxton punk ass walks off leaving Melania.

"Guess he had enough of your stinky shit." I smile.

"He'll be back," she says confidently.

"Landon, like you can talk. Another one left you? Just like Paul, shame. Yours don't come back." Ty flings her long brown hair over her shoulder.

"You got me confused, hooker. Do I look like I care? Unlike you and your hoe partner, I go for quality not quantity. I don't bend over or spread them for anything with a dick. I have a real career that doesn't require stretching my pussy for pennies."

"Whatever. While your lonely ass is home alone, Marcus will keep me company," Ty says proudly.

I laugh. "You're dumber than I thought. You seriously that chick that needs to keep her mouth shut. You're bragging about picking up a fool I don't want, basically threw out. You picked up my garbage. Stop emulating me. You will never get anywhere close to my level. The best thing you can do is just admire."

"Bitch, please. You wish. Nothing worth admiring," Melania said before going to sit next to Braxton with Ty following right behind like a puppy dog.

Melania rubs her hand on Braxton's chest and whispers something in his ear that causes him to smile. I can tell by the glimmer in his eyes it's something sexual. These two…I wanted to slap the hell out of both of them.

I had one more thing left to say. I walk over invading their space. "Make sure you use three condoms. These bitches crotches are always in operation, so many in and out. Who knows what germs you'll catch. I wouldn't want you catching anything. And definitely don't want you spreading anything." I gave him a death stare.

Yeah I was going to have to break this shit up with Yassy's ass. My loyalty is to Yasmin. Mothefucker, it's on.

8

Tainted Love

When I arrive to Mommy and Daddy's, I see a brand new white Mercedes S63. My mother is in the study in one of her law books. I admire my mommy for a few minutes, still flawless, size four as always. Only difference is that now she wore her hair in a short do. The smell of the dinner I picked up caused her to look up.

"How's my gorgeous baby?"

"I'm wonderful Mommy. Nice car. Daddy bought you another 'I'm sorry' present?"

"Actually no, I bought that myself."

"Don't tell me daddy's been on his best behavior?"

"I would say that. I haven't seen anything, but I don't look for these things. His responsibility is to keep our brand respectful. I'm so over your father's shenanigans."

"You are?" My daddy hasn't been the best husband or role model for me, but I didn't necessarily want to see my parents divorced. Weirdly, I've become accustomed to this craziness.

"Let's go into the family room."

My parents French style home was decorated with hues of cream and gold, very elegant and luxurious.

"So what's going on with my baby? How's life treating you?"

"Everything is going well. Business is growing. I had two settlements this week and I have five next week."

"It's wonderful that business is going so well. How are the men treating you?"

"My men are good. One is a little too good."

"Are you talking about Will? He is a cutie."

"Oh no, his time is coming to an end. He is annoying."

She laughs. "Who is the one that is a little too good?"

"He's too perfect. I mean he's not the norm at all. I'm waiting for the asshole, excuse my French, to come, but he's holding steady. Trying to figure out his game."

"Is my baby catching feelings?"

"I know mommy, don't be mad. I haven't even had sex with him. I refuse to until I get these emotions under control. He really is persistent."

"Who is he so I can do a thorough investigation on him?"

"His name is Eric Ayres. He plays center for the Washington Wizards."

"I must meet this Eric."

"Are you mad?"

"No, baby. You are human and you are so sweet. It's natural for you to catch feelings. I just want you to be cautious and when you do settle, not to settle for anyone. Just like I told you before, don't let your heart overrule your common sense."

"What made you fall for daddy?"

"You father is very charming. He was ambitious. He made me feel empowered. We both knew what we wanted, knew we would get it too. In law school, we clicked, worked well together, we were feared. It felt good having power." I see a faint smile along with tears she refused to allow fall from her eyes. She rapidly blinked them away.

"You have me," I say to try to lighten her sad state.

"Yes, I do. You will always be my best accomplishment. You never can have it all. My life isn't perfect, no one's is, but I have a wonderful life."

She talked a good game. Years of being a lawyer taught her well, but I could tell from the look in her eyes, each infidelity hurt like the first. It never got easier and pride would not allow her to leave, appearances meant too much. At least she knew what she was getting with daddy. Her way of coping was making him pay her way. For me, I knew love would never do, never fall. Landon and fool would never be together. I learned to get mine and never play the fool.

"How did you become immune to daddy?"

"Honestly, I don't focus on it. I have so many other projects going on. If I do feel myself getting sentimental, I remind myself of why I shouldn't."

"Do you still love daddy?"

"I have love for you father."

"Mommy you aren't answering my question."

"Landon I always try to be as honest as I can be with you. I stopped asking myself that question years ago. I am content with the ways things are. Are you asking these questions because your feelings for Eric run deeper than you will admit?"

"I admit I have feelings, but love, no. No offense, but you and Yasmin are the reinforcement I need not to go down that road."

"How so?"

"Mommy I lived this façade with you. Daddy

portrays the role of devoted, loving family man to the public, but behind the curtains he does his own thing."

I see the hurt in Mommy's face. I didn't mean to sound so callous but she knew it was the truth.

She sighs, I continue.

"Yassy has gone stupid for this guy named Braxton. He's cute, but not gorgeous. She can do much better. His money is decent but not on the level she should be getting. She's thinks she's the only one he's with, but I saw him a few nights ago with this trifling groupie. I said something to him and you know what the cocky punk said?"

"What?"

"He told me to tell her. He knew she wasn't going anywhere. It pissed me off because he is right. I hate seeing my girl being used or looking like a fool."

"Poor thing. She has to find out on her own though, Landon. You can't save her."

"I can help guide her into the light."

She gives me a doubtful look.

"I'm still going to try to help my girl. This will help me get my emotions together. Show me why I don't want a serious relationship. I will not be going that route."

"It's not always that easy. I know I've drilled in you to stay away from love, but my dear I see you falling."

"I won't."

"Well, as a precaution if you ever marry, always keep a stash. When the time comes and you're married I will show you how to hide your money."

"Do you ever think you will divorce daddy?"

"I don't know."

"So you have thought about it?"

"I have but men are men. It's not right, but your father isn't terrible.

"Yeah, I guess you're right."

A commercial came on for Governor Hemsley's re-election.

"That is one sexy old man," I comment.

"He isn't old. Just a few years older than me."

"He's nice looking. I wonder…"

"Wonder what?"

"If he looks as good without the clothes and if he needs Viagra."

"Landon," mommy says appalled.

"I'm sorry just curious."

"Are you still working on his campaign?"

I see a twinkle in Mommy eyes, "Yes, I am."

Mommy didn't look a day over 35. She always received plenty of male attention, but I never saw her respond or accept her many propositions. As far as I knew, she was committed to daddy, but you never know. However, I do know Mommy and Governor Helmsley always had a close relationship. Judging from the twinkle in her eye, hmm. I say, 'O yeah, mommy good for you. Daddy shouldn't be the only one to have all the fun.'

9

So Gone

"Hey Yassy," I sang into the phone when she picked up.

"Hey Diva. How are you?"

"I am very well."

"That is definitely good to hear. I was missing my Diva."

"Well you should have called."

"I did call you last week and two days ago. You told me you were in the middle of something and would call me back."

"Oh, well I am now. I haven't hung out with my bestie in a while. I miss my Yassy too, we should go out.

Yasmin laughs, "Yes diva. We should. Where do you want to go?"

"Well Will is having a party, we can go there. There will be plenty of opportunity. We can have some fun, tease some guys."

"Landon you know I'm not trying to date anyone. I'm with Braxton."

"I said tease. I didn't say date. You and Braxton's relationship is still new. Stop being so serious too soon. Take your time. You're still young."

"We're good."

"Yas, he is a wannabe pimp."

"Landon, he is not a pimp. Stop being so dramatic."

"Yassy, I am delivering to you truth. You're drinking that concoction that will have you singing 'You Made A Fool Of Me'."

She sighs, "Landon."

"Is he only dating you? I mean seriously, has he told you you're the only one he's fucking or going out with?"

"No, but he calls me practically all day. We go out like four times a week. His dick can't get enough."

I roll my eyes like she can see me. Her ass is so clueless and infatuated it's ridiculous. "Well it isn't official. You shouldn't limit your options and settle just yet."

"Landon, I'm not settling," she says, offensively.

My girl can't see the forest for the trees. I can't take her being so weak and naïve. I breathe in. I want to slap some common sense in her. Especially after that cocky motherfucker had the nerve to make those comments, I give up for now. "You're right, but we can still go to the party. It will be fun."

"I do miss my diva time. When is the party?"

I smile, "Tomorrow. I will pick you up around eight. Don't dress conservatively. Yas, loosen up. I can come pick out your outfit if you want."

She laughs, "Landon, I will pick an outfit that you will approve of."

"Can I suggest you show some skin?"

"You can, but I'm not listening. I will wear what I feel like."

"Great a potato sack."

"I'll make sure to wear a scarf with it to cover my face."

"Bye, Yasmin," I hung up the phone.

Yasmin actually surprised me. Her outfit was cute. She chose a liquid legging showing off her thick thighs and butt and zippered shirt, showing off her cleavage. I immediately gave my girl a hug for making me proud. I chose mini skirt with white top.

"Hey Landon," Will approached giving me a hug.

"Hello Mr. You remember my friend, Yassy?"

"Hello, Miss Yasmin. How have you been?"

She scans his new home, "Well, thanks. Nice place."

"Your girl hooked me up. Got me a good price too."

"Yes, she is good at her job," she compliments me.

"Yasmin, as you see, the bar is over there. Drink, mingle, have fun."

We walk over to the bar and have a few drinks. I have the Ginger and Grand Marnier. Yassy orders peach coconut Ciroc and pineapple. We chat a little while I scan the room looking for a dance partner for Yassy. Will came over to get me for a dance and I took a break from my hunt to oblige him. Four songs later, he still had me on the dance floor. Yassy was still in the same spot.

I wish Yasmin would learn to loosen up. She was at the bar looking uncomfortable, thinking of that asshole no doubt. I end my dance with Will and go to Yas.

"Yas, you look so bored, drink up."

"I am bored."

"Well, have a drink and let's dance."

She gave me that 'I'm not in the mood' look. I ignored it and ordered us both drinks.

It took a few drinks, but Yassy finally began to loosen up. We were on the dance floor and before I knew it she was dancing with Shawn Hayes, a player for the Atlanta Falcons. When I looked over again she was intertwined with Dante Palmer. He played in the NFL for the Washington Redskins. He was average looking, nothing sexy, but I hope his personality got my friend's attention. She was laughing which was a good thing.

I decided to focus on Will.

"Will it's been a while since I've talked to you. What's going on with you? Anything new?"

"Nope."

"Your party has a nice crowd. Will this be an all-nighter?"

"It can be for us."

"I have my friend maybe next time," I lied.

"You are turning me down? You got all the women's envy."

"What?"

"Landon, how does it feel to be out with a star? I could pick anyone in the room, but you got lucky. How do you plan on thanking me?"

I had to give it to Will for being straight up, but his tact, no. No he did not know who he was talking to. He still didn't realize I was not the one. "Will you are the lucky one. I could be with anyone. I'm with you because you were convenient. You are what I refer to as a starter, just something to settle the craving before the main dish. If this were an event, you would not even be a headliner. You are someone that will be forgotten. You are the reason you show up late for a show. You are a simply a filler."

"What?"

"Alright, Will," I started to add something, but thought why.

I walk off, heading for Yasmin. When I get to her, she looks like she is two seconds from going off.

I hear Dante say, "Dem thick thighs around my waist, I'll fuck you all the time. You think you can handle all this dick?"

Yasmin rolled her eyes, "I don't want to handle your dick. Me fucking you was never or will ever be an option."

I wanted to punch this motherfucker myself. She didn't need this and he was fucking up my damn plan. Damn, another gold star for Braxton's arrogant ass. These assholes make him look like a god compared to these cocky ass overrated NFL players. Too many hits to the brain got them on some delayed retard shit. We need to switch sports.

"Oh, so you trying act like you don't want the dick?" Dante retaliates.

"No, acting. Goodbye, Dante."

"We don't have to fuck. You can suck my dick."

I pull her over to the bar before it got out of control. "Yassy, let me introduce you to Mark Evans. He plays for the Detroit Pistons. He…"

She cut me off. "Landon, I really don't feel like being bothered. Dante and Shawn were annoying, arrogant and a hot mess."

I couldn't really argue with that, but I tried. "Yassy I give you that, but don't let them ruin your fun. Let's dance."

"Diva, you can dance. Enjoy yourself. I will go sit at that bar. You got 30 minutes and then I'm ready to go."

No hook-ups or potentials for Yassy. My night wasn't any better, especially since I cut Will. I need a replacement soon because me dating Eric exclusively was not a good thing.

10

Certainly

"How's business?"

Javon comes into my office, taking a seat in front of me. Javon was Braxton's best friend. I knew him prior to Yasmin hooking up with Braxton. We ran in the same circle, so I saw him often. I recently sold him a penthouse on Virginia Ave. in D.C.

"It's great."

"That's good."

"Would you like to add some more property to your portfolio?" I raise an eyebrow.

"Possibly."

"What's preventing that 'possibly' from being a yes?"

"Nothing."

"I will make it happen. Do you want to purchase a property in the Maryland or Virginia area?"

"I have a business partner who needs property."

"Ok, what, he was scared to come?"

"No, not at all. I just wanted to talk to you first, see where your head is at."

"Javon, what's up with the riddles? You know I handle my business. If you weren't satisfied with my services you wouldn't be here," I say with confidence.

"You do. My partner is looking for something on a larger scale. He's very particular. He also likes to entertain. Do you think you can handle that?"

"I like to be entertained. Sounds like my type of client."

"I will set up something with Rocco, do a formal introduction."

"I look forward to meeting, Mr. Rocco."

*

I'm actually excited to see Eric, even more surprised that I missed him. Being around Eric allowed me to unwind, relax. Or maybe it's his head game, just wonderful. Oh, how heavenly, to sipping white zinfandel, letting his tongue work its magic on my clit. Besides that, I really did enjoy his company.

"Hey, sweetheart," Eric greets me with a kiss on the cheek.

"Hello, handsome. I missed you." I step aside to allow him into my Chatsworth townhome.

"You miss me? I'm surprised."

"Why do you say that? You're making me feel like I don't show you enough. I guess I have to prove it you." I give him my sincerest look.

"How do you plan on doing that?"

"I'd rather show you."

"Really? His curiosity piqued.

"First, I cooked dinner for you."

Skepticism all over his face, "You cooked? For me?"

"I warmed up for you."

"I thought I smelled something. Thought it was coming from your neighbor's house."

I giggled. "No, here for you."

"Good. I'm hungry. Hope you bought enough. You know I like to eat.

"I did. I do."

Thanks to Vidalia restaurant, Eric's menu consisted of roasted monkfish, low country Frogmore stew, salad, paired with Sauvignon Blanc.

I leave him alone for fifteen minutes to fix his plates.

"I'm waiting," he calls out.

I walk in with the tray of food as he puts his hands behind his head and lies back on the couch.

Sitting the tray on the table, "Wait no more."

Continuing to create a sensual ambience, I put on some contemporary jazz. Taking a seat next to Eric, I relaxed in the chair watching him enjoy his meal. My mind drifted, Eric was muted, and I was savoring everything.

"You weren't hungry, sweetheart?"

"Not for food. Are you ready for dessert?"

"Only if it's you," he says pulling me in his lap.

Kissing his lips was always welcomed. The softness, the sweetness stirred me every time. Forcing myself away, I stand only to strip completely naked. Eric's pants off on the floor now, his dick erect, summoning me to taste the flavor. I walk to him, turn around giving him ass. He kisses it. Then he bites my left butt check. I feel a wave of pleasure throughout my body. I break away. Climbing on the couch, I saddle up and tongue him down. Then I turn so my back is against his stomach, knees still on the couch. I bend forward lift my legs placing one on each side of his head, resting my knees on his shoulder conveniently resting in a 69 position. Feet on the headboard of the sofa, I ease my pussy on his tongue and let him relish the taste. Let's see how many licks it takes Landon to get to the top. My mouth forms the letter O, as his dick glides all the way down my throat. Soon the suctioning begins, up, down, down, down, so erotic. I push more pussy in his face so I can take a lick of his dick, my candy. I suck him in holding his dick firm while my tongue circles the center. He sucks my clit. Then he nibbles so lightly it almost tickles. I let go letting the juices from my mouth cover his dick. I go in again sucking him like I'm bobbing for apples. Being upside down giving me another level of intoxicating desire, I'm on a high so dizzy from pleasure and the lack of oxygen. Eric explodes in my mouth. I drink his nectar like it was a sweet coconut smoothie that I couldn't get enough of. Which I couldn't, I wanted, needed more, but not tonight.

*

Rocco reeked power, money, his vibe turned me on. He was Italian tall with dark eyes, straight jet-black hair and smooth olive skin. I knew he had a dark side and for me, it only added to his appeal. I know cliché, he just turned me the hell on. Assessing the imprint in his pants, he wanted to get to know me in a familiar way. Javon introducing me to Rocco turned out to be a very good thing. Rocco was the diversion I needed from Eric. Even better, he had the means to make me very wealthy. Rocco's impulsiveness was always welcomed, which explained why we were naked on the kitchen counter of a property I was supposed to be showing.

"Landon, I love the feel of your lips. You are so sexy. Your lips are sweet, tastes like cherry.

I smile. I have something else sweeter.

"Is that so?" He licks his lips.

"You should taste me. Just imagine… Sweet pussy on your lips, taste just like honey. "

"You are a naughty girl."

"I am a horny girl. Can you make me cum? Will you make me? Come taste this honey, let me put this honey on that tongue of yours. You won't be able to get enough and then I will smother your dick with all with my juices. But first, I think I want some milk, I say circling my tongue around his dick."

"Ahh," he moans. "Business with you is always a pleasure.

11

I Only Want to Give it to You

I will not fall for Eric. He will hurt me in the end because all men cheat. Purposely avoiding Eric was not working. Even my business meeting with Rocco couldn't cure my yearnings. Today's struggle was no better since he showed up to my house in a white Ferrari bearing a gift.

"Hello, sweetheart."

I love presents. I take the beautifully wrapped box and delicately tear it open. Landon doesn't do thirsty. Inside was a key, he is so lame. I try not to frown, but I couldn't help it. On the brighter side, this corny, overbearing Eric, I didn't like. He turned me off. Bring it!

"You're disappointed?"

I lie, "No, I'm just confused. A key, this relationship is new and I don't want to rush. I think we need to get to know each other more. Accepting this key is like saying we're taking the next step."

He chuckles. "Landon, I would like nothing more than to get serious with you, but I agree. We have a long way before we can commit."

"Oh, so this joke's on Landon? Are we playing games?" I ask defensively.

"No, not at all. The key was to represent the world is yours."

"I know this."

He laughs. "You definitely do. You are so confident and independent it's a turn on." His sexy black diamond eyes twinkle. Let me finish, Ms. Independent. I could have given you jewelry or other materialistic items, but you get that all the time. I want the key to open up that heart of yours. You put on a good front, but I know it's a front."

I was about to respond but he shushed me.

"Landon, there's something about you that attracts me to you. I like your vibe and your spunk. I could have bought you a gift and I will," he winks. "I want to get to know the real Landon. The one who opens up and without the make-up.

"That's a privilege and you have to do more than give me a key if you expect me to open up."

"It is a privilege and I wouldn't want you to just open up. No worries, I will earn my way in."

"Oh, really," my eyebrows raise.

He grabs me around the waist, "I will."

One thing he got right, I love a man who is aggressive with going after what he wants with a side of confidence. Two stars for Eric. Damn.

"Come on, sweetheart. Let's go.

"Go?"

"Yes, I want to show you something."

Eric drove to the airport.

"Where are we going?"

"I have a surprise for you," Eric smiles.

"And what would that be?" He definitely had me intrigued.

"I want to take you away and spend time with you. Break through that shell of yours and show you I'm all that you need."

"Oh, so you think so?"

"I know so, Landon aka Ms. Independent. I know that you like the best, and you purchase the best. What you want you get, but I am who you need. All that you need."

"What makes you think that you are who I need?"

"I've been watching you."

"Whoa, whoa, you sound like a stalker," I say seriously.

He laughs, "I don't."

"I'm not following you or anything crazy. I observed your mannerisms. When I say I'm watching you, what I mean is, Landon, I see you. How you walk. How you talk. It says I am confident, gorgeous, invincible. I like that."

"We've established that." I tilt my head letting him know I meant it.

"You are confident, most definitely gorgeous, but you're not invincible." He pauses and looks at me with seriousness. "Landon I want to be that person that you relax with. Let go of the façade. I know you tired. I want to be that person you can trust. Be that person you let in that heart you built a wall around to protect."

I give him the look back. "Yeah it sounds good. You talk a very good game. But actions speak louder. My heart is a very valuable thing. I don't give it away. You haven't done anything extraordinary to make me want to offer it to you." I pause. "This trip is nice, but like you said. I could have done this myself. Furthermore, there is no façade. I am all that you said and more," I wink.

"You're right. The proof is in the action. Obviously, you don't know a real gentleman or man that is genuine. I am about to treat you like the queen you are," he says before literally sweeping me off of my feet.

Eric reserved a private plane to fly us to a secluded destination. Once boarded on the plush plane, which was furnished nicely in cream leather seats, wood grain accents, I exhaled. My body melted into the sofa leather. I wanted to take in the view from over the states enjoy the luxury of the plan, but I was blindfolded. Eric reclined the chair back, took off my shoes and began to gently massage my feet.

"Are you looking forward to the holidays?" I randomly ask.

I don't celebrate the holidays because it is like saying that's the only day you should give acknowledgement. People go all out for one day and the next day it's back to the same old thing."

"That's an interesting way of looking at it, but one day is better than none," I giggle. "Seriously though, your birthday is one day a year. Most people do that day. I like to celebrate every day like it's my birthday, but in my birthday month of November, I am so extra. My actual birthday is on November 18th."

"I know that's why, I like you. You don't limit yourself. You go get what you want."

"Exactly, I was taught young not to sit and wait for things to happen, make them happen." I sigh.

"That's right, both of your parents are attorneys."

"You remember."

"I told you, I pay attention. How was that life?"

"What do you mean?"

"What is your favorite childhood memory? What was it like living with your parents?"

I thought for a moment. "My favorite memory, I don't know, I never thought about it."

"You can't tell anything good about your childhood. Cousins coming over, family reunions, birthday parties, school."

"I am an only child. I didn't see much family growing up. My parents moved away from both sides. It was just me. My parents are also lawyers, so a lot of times they were in the office. They kept me busy in ballet, dance, and any activity I seemed interested in. I never wanted for anything, so I was lucky."

"So school, being around other kids wasn't fun?"

"I wouldn't say all that. I was in private school until tenth grade. Private school, at least the one I attended, was too structured and boring. The other kids were stiff. I convinced Daddy to transfer me to public school in tenth grade. That's when the fun began. There were rules, but not like private school, no uniform and boys," I laughed.

"How did you convince your father to transfer you?"

I left out the incident with Jason. "I told him I wanted be around people I could relate to. I felt like I had no connection. I needed street smarts to go into business. At that time, my parents thought I would follow their footsteps, go into law. Truthfully, I never had that desire."

"I definitely can't imagine you as a lawyer."

"I can argue, but the research behind it, never was for me. I hate research. Transferring was the best thing."

"So you do have something you remember from your childhood, albeit late. What's the best thing about high school?" He alternates massaging my foot.

"Definitely meeting Yasmin, there was hesitancy on her part because she is so reserved, but we clicked. Yasmin, I know I can count on no matter what. She needs to loosen up granted, however, she is a genuine friend, like a sister."

Eric began telling me more about him. "Landon, I grew up in Marietta, Georgia. My parents were married for thirty-seven years. She died two years ago from an aneurysm."

I remove my foot and reach for an arm, hand. "I'm so sorry to hear that Eric."

"Thanks. My father died three months later of what old people say was a broken heart. My grandmother is still alive, I make it a point to call her once a day and visit her twice a month. I have an older brother, but he's – out there."

I attempt to remove the blindfold so I could give him a hug, but he stops me. "I want you to relax. You are allowing me into your world. I just want to let you into me. No need to be sad. I've accepted their death. It is a part of life."

"It is, but I don't like it. I just want to give you a hug."

He pulls me up from my seat, places me in his lap, and hugs me. "You never had anyone close to you die?

"No, it's only been me and my parents. My grand-parents both died before I was seven. I don't really have any memory of them. Neither one of my parents are close with their siblings. I only see other relatives every few years."

"Wow, that's sad."

"I can't miss anything I never had."

"Family, as crazy as they can be, is important. I make it a point to see my aunts and uncles throughout the year. They're all I have. They are a part of who I am."

He removes the blindfold. "So, sweetheart do you like what you see?"

Instantly, I'm greeted by a sign welcoming us to Aruba. I stood there entranced in the scenery of palm trees, water of the prettiest blue. The aroma in the air filled with exotic flowers, sea salt, for me was orgasmic. The temperature, perfectly hot, I wanted to strip, roll in the sand and just bask in all the luxury bestowed be-fore me. Our oceanfront penthouse was adorned with a banquet of flowers, fruits, champagne. The private balcony had a captivating view of the ocean to enjoy Aruba's beautiful sunsets.

"Yes, darling, perfect." I pull him down into a passionate kiss. For his outstanding gesture and creativity, it was time for him to experience my extraordinary jewel. Fondling his dick stimulated him the way I wanted.

Eric snatches me up. Somehow he manages to unbutton his pants, move my thong aside and dive into my jewel in consecutive swift motions. I wrap my legs around his waist, receiving all of his remarkable inches. He backs me into a wall, fucking me hard. My arms wrap around him, holding on tight. I dribble off his dick like I am his basketball, the speed increasing as if he running down the court. Thump, thump, thump, thump, thump, thump, thump, thu-thump damn, double dribble, a violation. My heart is thumping . Thump, thump, thump, thump, thu-thu-thump, another violation, thu-thu-thu-thump, triple, thump, thump, thu-thu-thu-thu-thu- thump. Got daamn, I orgasm.

He slows things down, carrying me to the enormous king size bed. There he teases me. First, he undresses us both, and then he sporadically places soft kisses over my body. He focuses again on my lips, his tongue explores my mouth, licking, nibbling, and sucking my bottom lip. He eases in me so slowly, I cry out in agony. Spreading my legs vertically, one up one down, in and out he goes. Slowly retracting, slowly. He stops postponing mine and his orgasm. The erotic kisses begin, he wants more. He takes both legs wraps his arms around them and pushes them back. He positions himself in plank position, I feel even more. The slow grind begins. He drills deep, steady, oh so powerful. Never thought an orgasm would make me cry until now. He hits that most sensitive spot, never allows me to get a grip, control my emotions. I let go, revealing all of my emotions, foregoing my façade.

Making love to Eric was dangerous. Whether fast and furious or slow and seductive, this man had me feenin'. The look in his eyes as he slithered in and out of me was hypnotizing. Many times, I tried to avoid his eyes, but he would force me to look at him. This feeling was way too intense, frightening, and the flutter in my heart too much to handle. His stamina never died. He sexed me morning, noon, and night. Our breaks in between allowed us to embrace the impressive scenery of the island making the connection between us inconceivably mind-blowing.

The last few days of the nine-day trip were difficult. I always had a sexual appetite. With the scenery, ambiance, and man, it was too easy to fall in love. If I have sex with Eric, I will be looking like Booboo the fool. All men cheat, but professional athletes are extra. I would be all in love thinking my pussy has him whipped. Whoa! Side note: my shit is good, and it is all that, but a man will try out some more just to verify he got the best. Yes, he'll come back, but I'm not for that, 'Oh you the only one.' Anh anh, you won't fool me. I love my Yassy, but seeing her ass is the epitome of why I cannot and will not fall. I will not let this heart lead me stupid. Daddy, Braxton, no other examples needed. Back to Aruba, the last two days of the trip, I lied and told Eric my period came. Eric was a sensational lover and he would have me singing stupid I love you phrases if I let him. Yes, I did the fake out PMS. Eric the gentleman wanted to just hold me, but I turned it up. Cramps, mood swing, I was evil. I hated to treat his gentle soul that way, but I had to look out for me. He eventually got the hint and allowed me space, deciding to sight-see on his own, which was wonderful. I made calls to the states arranging a date with Rocco. I had to get him out of my system.

12

I Don't Want To

I hung out with Kevin and his little friend, Nicole. I recently sold him a townhouse. I wanted to check out his style. My impression of his masculine-styled home with dark walls, brown leathers accented with bamboo and cherry wood pieces was typical, yet nice. Nicole? Something was off with her. She was too quiet. Yassy is quiet, but this chick right here, something is off with her. She was cute. I had to laugh because, with the exception of the eyes and naturally long hair, she was a Yasmin clone. Yassy was far prettier, this version was cosmetically enhanced. Yassy has a better figure too. I know from watching Kevin salivate over Yassy's big breasts, his preference, Nicole was definitely lacking. Even my petite pretty self had more.

Nicole was eyeballing me conspicuously. I was two seconds from asking if she was bisexual. I would be nice and politely tell her if that floats her boat, fine, but Landon loves the dick.

"So Nicole, how is Kevin treating you?"

"Well…"

"Do you like his new place?"

"Yes."

"Do you live in the area?" I asked so over the top.

"Yes."

Everything in a monotone voice driving me crazy. Ok, she is too secretive. I'm trying to feel her out, get a sense. I swear something's up with this chick. Shoot I'm just going to be blunt.

"Do you talk other than one-word answers? What do you do for fun? Any personality in there? You killin' me over here?"

"Landon," Kevin warned

Kevin should know by now.

"I am always direct, Nicole. I do apologize if I offended you. I was just trying to get a conversation going. It's boring in here."

"No problem," she says meekly.

"Well, I got two words from you. I guess that's progress."

Nicole gives a fake laugh, "It just takes me a while to warm up."

"Yeah."

Focusing my attention on Kevin, "So Kevin what are we going to do for Yassy's birthday?"

I look over at Nicole unreadable stiff, let me see if she's jealous. "Have you met Yassy, Nicole?"

"Briefly."

Here we go with these one word responses. "She's gorgeous isn't she? Her, Kevin and I go way back."

"Yeah, that's what Kevin said."

"Are you coming with us?"

"No, I have a prior engagement."

Yeah, she's jealous. She must see the way Kevin stares at her. Little does she know that feeling was not mutual. These two were putting me to sleep. I excused myself to call Eric.

"Landon, I had enough from you. I tried coming at you straight with no games. I thought you were finally seeing that I am not going to hurt you."

"Eric, I never promised you or told you that you were the only one I was seeing."

Eric was having a tantrum because since returning from Aruba, I've limited his time. We hooked up a few times for some sexual healing, but it was brief. He wanted me. I just couldn't give him that.

"You know what Landon, I'm not going to keep playing this game with you. Your mood swings, your attitude."

"I'm not playing games. I am very direct."

"Your back and forth, running in and out of my life. I'm tired of it. Make up your mind and stick with it."

"Are you done?"

"Yeah, I'm done with this shit. Bye, Landon."

"Have a nice day, see you later."

"So damn condescending. I'm not in the mood for this bullshit. You pissed me the hell off. This shit is not a game."

"Why are you acting like a bitch? All I said was have a nice day."

"Landon, enough of the bullshit."

13

Put It Down

It's no secret I like the finer things. I believe in doing things big, enjoying life to the fullest. Why should I settle? I love sex, my body, men. No offense. I am glad to be a female. Because I love dick, it comes in so many sizes, variety. I only deal with the magnum though. If I were a male I probably would be gay. Humping and licking vajayjay is not my thing. If you like, hey, do it well. I like the interaction and the feeling you get when the dick slides in you. A dildo will give you a false sense. An imitation will be good for a while, but again there's nothing like the real thing. I like to squeeze a dick, pull it out, tease. I drive the men wild that way. I can't do that with a dildo.

Scanning the lounge I see all the conformation I need to as why I should not settle with Eric. Today just may turn out to be a good day after all. Needing a drink after multiple showings to come up with nada my intent was to go home and do just that. Rocco called me as soon as I arrived home. I explained that I didn't feel like driving. Not a problem, Rocco sent his driver. I headed to Indulgence lounge. I waste no time approaching Rocco who is sitting on the sofa, waiting. He is impeccably dressed as usual. His top two buttons loose on his white shirt. Suit dark, tailored to fit only him, Versace

Medusa Velvet slippers, Rocco's appearance screamed money, power.

"Hello, Rocco."

"Landon, have a seat."

"How are things?"

"They're well. How is business for you? The markets down, not many buyers." He says matter-of-factly.

The business proposal Rocco offered seemed decent. I stood to make six figures or more. Problem was his expectations were undesirable.

"I don't like your terms."

"We can negotiate. What do you want?" Rocco says.

"A bigger percentage of course, I am taking a huge risk."

"Anything else?"

"Yes, Melania. I want her out."

"Neither one of those are negotiable."

"Excuse me?" I say pissed that he dismissed my request so quickly.

"You heard me."

"You said we could negotiate. What else is left to negotiate?"

"When you put it like that, you're right. Those are the terms."

"I don't trust Melania. I can't work with anyone I can't trust."

"You're not getting into a personal relationship with her."

"I don't care. I don't like her. I don't want to be affiliated with her in any way. I dealt with her in the past and she messed up my money."

"Business is business. You will not actually have any

contact with her. I deal with her as I do with you. There is no reason for you to contact each other."

"She can't run a business. The only thing she can run is to the clinic."

"Your vendetta, jealousy or whatever it is does not affect my business. Comprende?"

"Jealousy? I'm not jealous of her. I don't trust her. She…"

"Like I said, this tiff you have does not affect my business. Make it work, get over it."

"I don't like your terms, so therefore I'm out. Find another partner."

"Landon, I don't play games."

"I'm not playing."

"Melania stays and the rate we agreed on stands."

"Effectively immediately our arrangement is terminated."

"I'm leaving," he stands.

"Well, bye." I flick him bye.

He gets up and leaves me without looking back. That Italian was going to regret giving me an ultimatum. How dare him. The worst part is that he leaves me stranded since he picked me up. I probably have to wait for an hour for a cab. I hated nasty cabs. Asshole. What is the name of a cab company? Well, at least I'm stranded here at Indulgence. It could be worse. Indulgence has a nice atmosphere of D.C. professionals. I could get a drink, find out a cab company.

Within minutes of sitting at the bar, I see Braxton sulking. Great, another asshole. Well this one I can get a ride from.

"Hello, Braxton."

He looks up and grunts, "Ok."

He's in a mood. I use my nice voice, "Hey Braxton, how are you?"

He forgoes the pleasantries, "What do you want Landon?"

"A ride."

"How did you get here?"

"A friend, but he had to go," I lied.

"The mouth got you stranded."

"So you were minding my business eavesdropping on my conversation?"

"Ease dropping? No, but your argument was heard because your annoying voice was so loud. I'm sure quite a few people heard you. Do I know word for word or care for that matter, no."

"Anyway, can I get a ride?"

"I'm drinking and I'm trying to relax."

Oh, he is an asshole. What Yassy see in him is beyond me. He irks me.

"Well Braxton, fiancé to my best friend, when you're done with your drink, can you please take me home?"

He takes a deep breath, "Alright."

I take a seat next to him and order a Victoria Secret, a concoction of vodka, peach Schnapps, Malibu rum, amaretto, and cranberry juice.

"You come here a lot?" I ask not really caring just trying to be cordial. I really wanted to find out about Yasmin, who just suffered a miscarriage, but the time and place wasn't the best. I figured that is more of a private conversation. I didn't know how he would react.

"No."

"What are you drinking?"

"Scotch."

"Eww, that is such an old man drink. You always drink that?"

"Landon, I don't feel like any conversation. I came here to get a few drinks, relax. Your questions, voice, are doing the opposite."

"I was just trying to be cordial, since I've been forced to deal with you."

"You know what, let me finish this drink and I'll take you home."

"That would be wonderful," I say sarcastically.

Braxton gulps down his drink, gets the bartender attention, orders another Scotch, and gulps that down. He leaves the bartender $50 to pay for both of our drinks and announces he is ready.

The ride to my house was only twenty minutes but each minute ticked like it was 30 minutes. I didn't bother to make conversation. Braxton never bothered to turn on the radio, just complete silence. It was dark I couldn't take in any scenery, a very long agonizing ride. I looked over to Braxton who looked to be in a trance. He looked worn, lost, deep in thought, drunk, I don't know. Either way I was at a loss. Didn't know what to say or do. I hated for him to leave here intoxicated, to run into something or somebody. I didn't want that on my conscience, Yassy would die if something happened and if I could prevent it I should. Against better judgment, I invited Braxton in, making up a story about him checking out something. Once he got out, I could tell he was alert and not drunk. It was obvious he had a lot on his mind. Inside he asked to use my bathroom. I took a seat at the counter. I was curious to find out how much of my conversation was overheard. More importantly, I wanted to know if he was involved in Javon's ventures. His ass could be trying to pimp my girl out. She wouldn't know. I know that was highly unlikely. He did put a ring on it and knocked her up. But you can't trust these guys and Braxton seems like the type to lose interest. My girl already going through it, I need to find out if he's still fucking with Melania too.

Fortunately, after his bathroom break, he looks more relaxed. I offer him some water. He asks for something stronger. I pour both of us a glass of cognac. Once he takes a few sips, I began my interrogation.

"So what did you hear me and my date arguing about?"

He takes a seat on the stool next to mine. "I don't know what you were arguing about, but the way Rocco left I know it wasn't a good date."

"I don't know what you are insinuating Braxton, like I said something came up. He had to leave."

He takes another sip. "Yeah, whatever Landon. You need to watch out. Rocco is not anyone to fuck with."

"And what do you know about Rocco?" I sip.

"Enough."

"What is enough?" I press.

"I know you need to watch it."

"Javon fucks with him."

"Javon deals with him on a different level. They do business together. And Javon can handle himself."

"What type of business?" I ask giving him a clueless look.

"I don't know all the details, something with financing and sales.

"You not in on it?" I press.

"No, I don't do business with friends."

"Oh. How's Yasmin?"

"Not good. She just mentally checked out. I don't know what to do or say to her."

"Yeah, me either. Do you want something else to drink?"

"Yeah."

I went to my bar, bringing back the cognac. I pour both of us another glass.

Braxton wastes no time drinking. "Every day she just lies in bed, balled up with a blank look in her eyes. No emotion."

"Poor Yassy. I tried calling her, but I always get the answering machine. I want to stop over, but I don't know what to say."

"She won't know you there. She barely acknowledges me. When she does, she cries and yells for me to leave her alone. I don't know what to do," his voice breaks.

I'm caught off guard he looks so broken. He looks like he is about to cry.

"Braxton, are you okay?"

Although he nodded his head yes, he wasn't. I've never seen a grown man so vulnerable. I went to hug him. It was very awkward. I definitely wasn't use to being in this position. This was a different affection. I remained still for a few minutes. When I pull back, my lips brush his neck. He looks at me and next I feel his lips touch mine.

The kiss we shared was the only one. From then on, everything was on fast forward, a blur, it was stripping to sucking. He pulled his pants down, I gasped. Nice just the way I like, long, thick and ready. Not as long as Eric's, but the girth, damn.

We move the couch and wasting no time, he enters me. I feel him stretching my walls. He moves my hips up and down, gliding in smooth like a criminal. Oh, yes.

On his lap, I begin a slow twirl with my hips. In a matter of seconds, he's up, and has me on my pretty marble counter. He pounds with force sending electric currents threw my body, each thrust my clit is tickled and singing praises. My orgasm comes quick and hard. My marble counter quickly becomes wet and slippery from the pleasure I was feeling. The force in combination with so much pleasure, was flooding the counter. I lose the dick. Eager for more, I wrap my legs tightly around his waist.

Braxton moves from the counter, my legs still securely wrapped with him inside, we descend to the floor.

"Unh, unh, unh, unh," are mutual grunts heard from both of us as he pounds me against my hardwood floors. Got damn, this shit feels good. Oh this motherfucker can go. I unwrap my legs from his waist and use my hands to pull my feet back. I wanted him to put all of it in me. He knows it and takes his hands to bend my legs all the way back. Oh shit! He is hitting that G-spot. Pound, pound, pound, slow stroke, pound, pound, pound, slow stroke, slow stroke, slow, long stroke, pound, pound, pound, pound, pound, ppppapound. Slow, slow, slow, slow, pound, slow, slow, slow, pound, pound , pound, slow, slow, slooooooow, pound, pound, pound, pound, pound, pppppppppound.

I can't take it. "Oh shit, oh shit, yes, yes, yes, Oh shiiiiit!" I scream like a crazed woman. My pussy is pulsating. Shit, I'm fucking pulsating!

I finally look at Braxton who still looks composed like he didn't break a sweat. I move my hips letting him know I was game for orgasm number three. He doesn't respond. Instead, he looks at me, shakes his head, sliding that magic wand he calls a dick out of me.

He stands, goes in the bathroom while I lay gloriously on the floor as reality begins to set in.

What the hell did I just do? I finally get up and take a seat on the chair. Damn, oh my god, Yasmin. Shit, shit, shit. I fucked Yasmin's man. How am I going to handle this? Is Braxton going to break up with my girl? Is he going to fuck both of us? That would not be happening. Good dick and all, Yasmin is my girl. I am not fucking her man while she's in lala land. This is so wrong on so many levels. What we just did, the ultimate betrayal. I will never fuck Braxton again after today. Damn I can't believe I just fucked him. What am I going to do? Ok how are we going to handle this? Think. Think. Think. I can't change what happened. I will forget this happened.

Braxton comes out the bathroom, magic wand swinging. I swear it put me in a spell. My mind was gone not thinking rationally.

Braxton looks at me, shoulders low, looking just as lost as me. I swear his dick was telling me to look at him and when I did it winked. Damn, I know I'm wrong for thinking this, but, Damn. I see why Yasmin ass is hooked. Braxton know how to make a pussy feel good. I feel like I'm in a trance. Damn, my shit is tingling now. I mean I know what we did is wrong it's not like we can change what we did. I need a last fuck. That dick was so got damn excellent. I know I'm not the only one to have the itching of an orgasm compromise logical thinking. I was in the moment. Oh, this is so wrong.

"What are you looking at?" He snaps.

I reach for him, he pushes me away. "You're done?" I knew my face looked confused.

"Hell yeah, the shit that just went down, shouldn't have happened." He says quickly dressing and I follow quickly covering my body.

"You right, it shouldn't have, but it did."

"I wish I would have just dropped you off and kept it movin'."

I shrug my shoulders. My orgasmic high completely gone. I know it seems fucked up and not genuine, especially after what just transpired, but I was really concerned for Yassy. I was scared he was going to break her fragile heart.

"Are you going to break up with Yasmin?"

"No!"

"So you're just going to fuck her? Have her think she's the only one you're fucking?"

"I'm not fucking anybody."

"You fucked me and Melania."

"Melania? I'm not fucking her. I stopped messing with her before Yasmin and I got engaged."

"I've seen you with her, Braxton."

"Landon, I love Yasmin. Yeah I fucked around, but when I put the ring on her finger that shit stopped. What just happened was a mistake."

"What do you mean fucked around?"

"You know what I mean. That was a long time ago before we got serious."

"Honestly?"

"Yasmin, damn Yasmin. She's going through too much. I can't believe I did this shit to her. Shit. Shit. Shit. She doesn't deserve this shit. I can't hurt her again. Yasmin." He berates himself. He put his head down, continually shaking his head no. Tears filled his eyes. I finally knew how he really felt.

"Oh, my god, you really do love her."

"What the fuck? This some fuckin' game you playin'?"

"Yes, I didn't think you were serious, especially after seeing you with Melania."

"Yes, I love Yasmin. I haven't been with Melania since the party. Yasmin and I wasn't serious back then. In the beginning, I didn't plan to get serious with Yasmin, but I do love her. I didn't propose for a game. I love her. All that shit before is in the past."

"Oh."

"Shit, how am I going tell her this? Damn! She's still struggling."

"Are you fucking crazy? You can't tell her."

"I don't want to, but I don't trust your ass. I need to tell her my way without you twisting shit to your advantage."

"Braxton, be for real. How the hell am I going to say, 'Yasmin I'm sorry I fucked your man. Forgive me.' Yes, Yassy puts up with a lot with me, but that won't be one. You and I will forget this happened."

"It's not that easy. I can't look at her especially as vulnerable as she is and lie."

"Which is why you can't say anything. If your conscience is that bad, then break up with her."

He looks at me with disgust, "You don't get it."

"I do get it."

"Well, how the hell you gonna tell me to break up with her like that? You think that's what the fuck I want to do? You think that's going make everything better? Did you not just hear me tell you I love her?"

"I didn't say it would be easy."

He shakes his head. "Yasmin's a good girl. How the two of you are friends, I don't get it."

"Excuse you, what the hell are you? Your dick has seen its share of pussy and landed in plenty of mouths. You are not a saint. Your numbers triple mine. Let's not talk about that hooker, Melania. Thank God you didn't give my girl any STD's messing with that skank."

"I can't take your mouth. I need to go."

"Bye."

"So neither one of us are going to say anything to Yasmin?" He confirms.

"No!"

Braxton is gone within a matter of seconds. I have really fucked up. How am I going to look Yasmin in the face? For now, I would be avoiding her ass until I got myself together.

14

$\mathscr{R}escue$ *me*

Five tests later, the results are the same. I thought I messed up before. This is even worse. Was this my punishment from up above? My ass is pregnant. I called the clinic. Sorry, but baby had to go. I sat in the chair as the doctor explained what I knew, I was terminating the pregnancy. Going in to do an ultrasound checking the baby's growth was the hardest. Although I tried not to look, I did. I saw a peanut. Inside that peanut was a little circle moving, heart beating, and I knew I couldn't kill a hopeless baby because I was careless.

Leaving the clinic, I thought long and hard about who the father was, Braxton or Eric? In Aruba, Eric and I didn't use protection 95 percent of the time, especially after the incident in the Jacuzzi. We sexed for hours without protection. I hooked up with him after my mishap with Braxton. Besides, I don't even think Braxton came. Eric was a strong possibility, Braxton not so much. It has to be Eric's. This baby was Eric's.

Eric would be a wonderful father and husband. Eric talked to me. It was more than sexual. Although I know he loved the sex, he was actually genuine when he asked how I was. He was interested in how my day went, cared when it was bad. He listened. He never asked for anything but me, appreciated how valuable time with me was.

Everyone reaction to my pregnancy was awkward. Telling my parent's was exhausting. Mommy thought I had lost my mind. My father knew better, he knew not to say a thing. Yassy was hurting over her miscarriage, but pushed her grieving aside to support me. Kevin thought it was a practical joke; it took him seeing to believe me. I remember how Braxton looked at my stomach and paused. I could see him praying what he saw wasn't real. He straight out asked was the baby his. I told him no, even though I knew and deep-down he knew, he was a possibility. He was persistent asking me several more times if I was sure. I assured him he was not. I also assured him I would never mention what happened between him and me to Yasmin.

Guilt was too much because two weeks later, Yassy called me devastated that she'd pushed Braxton away. I felt like crap, I couldn't admit that I was part cause. I did the only thing I knew to do, tell her he was crap and she deserved better.

Of course I was scared to tell Eric. He had enough of my indecisiveness in regards to our relationship. Pregnancy hormones must have really affected me. Hearing his voice had me vulnerable. I realized I missed him. Telling him wasn't as nearly as bad as I thought it would be. Eric was elated. Eric moved me into his place, taking care of all my wants. It came to no surprise to anyone when he proposed. We both agreed, the place our baby was created would be where we were married.

Eric spared no expense making sure it was a fairy-tale. Yassy and Kevin by my side along with my parents. Contrary to what everyone expected me to do, I chose small and intimate. There were a few of his family members making slurs throughout the ceremony. He wasn't lying when he said his family was crazy. Prior to getting married, every time we were together, either his cousins or aunts and uncle were calling for money. I met them twice, once at an uncle's 50th birthday party and the second, when his grandmother had complications in the nursing home. She didn't say much, but she always had her eye on me, like she was studying me, checking to see if I was worthy of Eric. Me being me, I smiled graciously, never showing uneasiness. His uncle and aunts were concerned about their asset Eric. They weren't feeling him getting married. They knew those family emergency funds were ending. I blocked them out, they weren't factors. The seven carat cushion cut diamond wedding ring was my favorite.

Married life wasn't all bad. Baby boy was awesome. Life was good except for Yassy. Months later, Yassy still was trying to get over her break-up. Seeing Yasmin sad eyes, identical to mine, got me each time. I couldn't take her pitiful lost look anymore. Giving Chauncey her number was a good move. Chauncey a ball player like Eric, had been crushing on Yassy for a while. Chauncey was tall, with smooth butter skin, thick curly hair, absolutely gorgeous. His dimples added to his sex appeal. They clicked and had been dating for a while.

Motherhood was an adjustment. I mean I instantly thought he was cute. It was the holding of a crying baby, trying to settle him down that got to me. Feedings, changing diapers, cleaning throw up, burping was hard for a chick like me. Eric really took care of everything. He handled everything, definitely earning father of the decade award. However, looking at the two together, I knew it was all a lie.

I won't lie, I lived the fantasy of a happy, loving family for a year…enjoyed it even. It was a different kind of feeling to be able to trust someone and know they love you. Daunting for me, I could not grasp or assume this sense of security would remain. There was an unbearable secret too detrimental hovering over my head. Mentally and emotionally, I had to prepare myself. Time was limited, I had to protect my assets, gain assets, and prepare for the worst. Mommy's words rang clear in my head, "Don't be a fool." Being vulnerable and weak was not a choice.

Until then I was going to enjoy the ride.

15

What You Want

Eric was too needy. He's very family-oriented. He wanted to take family trips to the museum, park, nature, history all that. Being an only child, I became accustomed to me time. He wanted me to bring little Eric to the games. A basketball game was too much for a one-year-old. I obliged, going to a few. Dealing with the player wives, wannabe wives, and groupies was taxing, resulting in quite a few verbal altercations. One of the player's wives, Lauren, hands me a set of rules on what the protocol was for the significant others at the game. Ever so kindly, I told her I don't take orders. Expressing to her, I was not a programmable Stepford wife, far from ordinary, thus will do as I pleased. That argument got very nasty and the only good thing was Eric stopped asking me to come to his games.

Little Eric was spending time with his God-Mommy Yasmin, Eric was on the road, and I was in my office going over some listings for a client. Eric was very frugal. He enjoyed the finer things, but he believed in a budget. He always stressed financial responsibility, planning for the future. He put away money for our son. He said once he was older, he was going to teach him about the stock market and growing money. He had plenty I knew, but he was on this is it a "need or a want." He said the way

I spend, we'd end up broke. He gave me a long lecture after I paid $40,000 for the Birken bag. I knew trading my Mercedes in for a Ferrari was a "No." Real estate was a lot of work. I hate paperwork and dealing with difficult clients. My clients were always challenging, often showing 20 houses or more before a contract was submitted. Then there was the back and forth with the inspection, the title company. I worked hard for the money that's why I dealt with houses of $500,000 or more. Honestly, with my taste, I should be in New York or L.A. showing multi-million dollar properties collecting commission. Eric's budget, along with my dismal sales, as of late, were not working. I had to get creative, make some money.

"Looking good, Landon," Javon compliments.

"Always." I sit next to him on the stool.

"Did you just come from showing property?"

"Why, are you looking for some property?"

"Perhaps in the future," he chuckles.

"What's so funny?"
"I think you want a piece of the action. I think you are regretting walking away from Rocco's

business proposal."

"I think you're an asshole."

"I know I am one."

I shake my head.

"I could talk to Rocco, if you make it worth it," he rubs his hand up my thigh.

"Javon, I must ask how involved Braxton is with your business."

"He's not."

"What does he know?"

"He knows I deal with the women, but not to the extent. He's been to some of the parties, the less risqué, he had limited access."

"Oh."

"Why are you worried?"

"He was fucking with my best friend. I don't want any shit to go down and she get caught in it,"

He laughs.

"What's so funny?"

"You acting concerned like you're the best friend in the world. "

"What are you talking about? I am concerned. Yasmin is my girl."

"That's why you fucked Braxton?"

My eyes widen in surprise. Why would that dumb ass motherfucker tell Javon of all people? "That dumb ass told you about that?"

"You know Braxton. Motherfucker got soft messing with ya girl. Got a conscience and shit. People like us, we know how to keep shit in the need to know. Divulge as little as possible."

I roll my eyes.

"Speaking of Yasmin, why don't you arrange something? I want a piece of that."

"Hell no, you stay away from her. " I say with a little too much conviction.

"Calm down. I was joking. I just like to fuck with her. Although, if by chance she does offer, I will take it. Those legs wrapped around me, I know will be a good thing."

"Javon, I'm serious. Yassy ain't built for this life or you."

"Yeah, yeah. So you going give me some or not."

"With a presentation like that, hell no."

"Landon, you know you hate the bullshit just as much as I do. We ain't doing no romancing. It ain't even on those terms. You like to fuck, I like to fuck. We don't get caught up in that romance. You know this. I don't know what's up with the dramatics tonight?"

"No dramatics over here. You just came at me way too foul."

"My bad," he holds his hands up in surrender.

"Javon, fortunately for you, I do have some tension. No fumbles tonight because I will embarrass your ass."

Javon took some of the edge off, but not enough. Meaning, he orally stimulated me. He got a hand job. I know how to accomplish that with these gifted hands.

What I really need to decide is if I want to get into bed with Javon and Rocco on a business level. Originally, when Rocco offered me the opportunity, I assumed we were just having plain ol' parties. But word spread that their parties were legendary. You see, Javon is a pimp. He is not a star on the line-up, meaning he's not getting bonuses of $125 million. He makes a decent amount, but the lifestyle he acquired requires more. He hustles another way. So calling Braxton a pimp was not far off. Granted, he's not one, but he hangs with a pimp and has sampled his share of product.

Javon felt cheated over our last encounter. He was all in his feelings. It's not my fault he didn't last two minutes. Well it is. He was dragging his feet about talking to Rocco. Luckily, I ran into Rocco at Ruth's Chris.

I take a seat at his vacant table. "You don't mind do you?"

Rocco looks me over, "I see having a baby didn't do any damage. Breasts are even fuller, nice."

I pat myself on the back for picking a low-cut violet color silk wrap dress.

"I see your eyesight is 20/20. You forgot who I am. I never disappoint."

"What about other parts. The baby didn't do any damage. Can I inspect?"

"No. Just know it's still nice, warm and wet. But I'm a married woman now."

"So I can't have a taste? A ride?" He asks sensually.

"Well I never say never, depends if we can agree to my terms. As of right now, I'm not intrigued."

"You summoned me, you must want something. What do you need? Or should I say, why are you entertaining me?"

"I saw you from across the room, you looked bored. I'm just being friendly. "

"Not bored, more like deep in thought."

"Obviously, you know what's going on with me since you mentioned my son. What are you up to, Mr. Rocco? How is life treating you?"

"Life is good, but I have a feeling you want to make it better."

"What gives you that impression?"

"Your eyes say you want something. My guess is money."

"Your guess is wrong," I lied. "I'm married to a very successful ball player who has an abundance of endorsements. Additionally, I have a very successful real estate business that deals with elite clientele. Landon has plenty."

"I don't believe it. You talk that talk. The real estate market took out a lot of key players, your clients. So that money is gone and let's be honest, you never was one to hustle for money in that game. Fortunately, for you, like you said, your husband has plenty. However, he isn't as generous with it, checks everything and you're bored. Nice guy, but too nice for you. You're the one that's bored."

"As I said before, your assumptions are wrong."

He chuckles. "Very good poker face."

"I don't play poker."

"The original offer stands."

I stand, "I'll give you my answer in 48 hours."

16

Diva

I knew better, but I ended up dancing with the devil. I conceded, agreeing to partner with Javon and Rocco to have sex parties.

For the next couple of weeks, I set up business programs and educational classes for real estate. Clients were instructed to use the access code "Income" when they wanted Javon and Rocco's services. For the individuals who really wanted home buying education, I hired someone to do webinars. So yes, I sat back and collected five figure checks, taking my cut. Later, I would in turn make deposits in various offshore accounts and non-profit charities run by both Javon and Rocco.

Being a licensed real estate agent, I have access to MLS listings and security codes to get into vacant homes. My responsibility in our partnership was to inspect properties. I do a walk-through with a technician hired by Rocco and Javon to sweep the property for security cameras. If any were found, the tech would disengage, and manipulate the camera so that everything appeared normal.

The preferable properties were selected on large secluded acres to prevent any unwanted paparazzi. Another must was a minimum space of 10,000 interior square feet. If the property met the criteria, I would rent it for

networking events, such as real estate seminars. I hired
stagers to make the home's décor inviting. The cleaning
crew made sure the mansion was spotless, linen was
fresh, house smelled of vanilla, sandalwood, and laven-
der. Attendees for the parties were thoroughly screened
by Javon and Rocco. If they passed the screening process they would contact me and pay fees ranging from
$10,000 to $50,000. The transaction would be charged
to my business. The customer's credit card would be
charged as a real estate education purchase.

Now the fees: $10,000 Bronze allowed you to look,
but don't touch; $25,000 Silver allotted you sexual
stimulation that would be performed in a voyeur room
and other selected areas of the house. The only drawback
was that all of the sexual activity on this level was visi-
ble to attendees. But, $50,000 Gold was no holds barred
and it allowed privacy. You could go anywhere, do anything: whips, chains, golden showers, bi, tri, whatever,
and no one but the participants were allowed to watch.
All attendees have to show ID to verify purchase. Then
they are given colored wrist bands based on the package
selected: $10,000 blue, 25,000 green and $50,000 red.

Melania's responsibility was to provide the escorts.
They are of different ethnicities, varieties ready to
please, and flawless from top to bottom. She's a good
stylist, I give her that. Upon entry to our parties, all cell
phones and cameras are turned over and a confidentiality agreement has to be signed. Awaiting the guests is a
buffet of oysters, clams, fruits, chocolates, and wine and
alcohol flowed freely. Large flat screen TV's throughout
the mansion. Each screen displaying different sex fetishes: bestiality, straight, gay, transgendered, hermaphro-
dite, bondage, etc.

Condoms are scattered throughout, but not a require-
ment. If you wish to partake in unprotected sex, HIV test
kits were administered by a doctor, but also not required.
Sexual stimulants such as arousal oils, erectile dysfunc-
tion drugs like Viagra and Levitra **were** made available.
Parties generally began at 8 p.m., lasting normally until

5 a.m. It wasn't uncommon for the parties to run through the weekend. Therefore, cleaning crews arrived promptly at 9 a.m. to thoroughly sterilize the property.

Parties were held twice a month, sometimes three for special occasions. On average, 150 people attended. Guest were professional athletes, models, actresses, anyone who had money to play. Each party was notorious. I've never partaken in any of the activities, but I enjoyed the show. Eric and I were barely on speaking terms, we cohabitated in different rooms. I never told him about my business venture and he didn't have access to my business account. Information on the parties was restricted, cameras prohibited, so the chances of him finding out about my involvement were slim. I did walk the mansions as the queen that I was, outfits were either tight, revealing, or both. I loved the attention. Not partaking increased the desire for me. Suitors eagerly gave me gifts to entice me, but I would respectively decline. Giving in would mean rescinding my power, I love power. Tease, I would continue to be.

Tonight, I decided to attend a movie premiere with Eric. Eric was actually the sociable one tonight, mingling, drinking. I decided to be reserved, still a little nervous, not use to seeing the freaky side of half the celebrities here. Although I couldn't talk due to confidentiality agreements, I knew. Unable to give some of these transgender lover celebrities a side eye, I practice something I was not familiar with, silence. So while I observed the guests, I got quite a few laughs.

Can't say I was surprised to see Melania claw all over Braxton. Hate to see my friend go through so much, but she is better off without him especially if he with that hoe. I know I like to have fun, but the bitch is sloppy and these dumbasses know she only out for the mullah. Braxton's even more disgusting, going from Yassy to this. Oh, I'm glad I hooked her up with Chauncey.

Although there's no love on her part, it was still a good thing. She shouldn't be falling in love anyway.

With Chauncey she's reaping the benefits, enjoying life like she should. My Yassy still not right, the way my girl was broke down after his ass broke up with her. But with the help of Chauncey and me, she will be lovely. He will regret doing her like that. Matter of fact, I need to contact Ebony magazine. Eric and I are featured as one of the hottest married couples, Yasmin and Chauncey can be a couple. My girl is on her business. She isn't a dummy or spreads her legs to earn her money like this hoe.

I know what it is though. The bitch got that vaginal surgery to tighten her shit to make it like a virgin. Tonya a messy gossiping queen whose husband played with Eric, told me. Her info was usually 99% accurate. If Melania did allow Braxton to fuck her it would be a dumb move. Braxton, asshole or not, has a nice big hammer that will relapse that shit. He got money, but not the eight figures she likes. If she was smart, she would go after the baseball profession. That's where the money is.

I observe the dumb ass. Yep, its official, she like the hammer. I shake my head as she runs her hand along Braxton's leg. Yep, she's about to waste all that money. She dumb enough to go for it. Pure comedy. His ass is looking annoyed. She looks hurt. I know this hoe don't have feelings for his ass.

I am sipping on my Chardonnay when Braxton approaches, I sigh.

"Landon."

"Braxton," I return.

"How is Yasmin? Is she ok? Is she happy? Does she need anything?" His eyes yearning.

My heart panged a little, he really did seem to be a desperate puppy dog, but him and Yasmin getting back together wasn't acceptable. Like I said, she can't go through that hurt again. The main key factor was little Eric. As my baby gets bigger, I see more of Braxton features. There was no way I could allow them back together and risk this coming out.

"Yes, Chauncey is making her happy."

"Are they really that serious?"

"Yes," I lied. "Braxton, you're going to have to move on. Ending things was the right thing to do. I know you didn't want to keep lying to her and you hated to see what it was doing."

He snaps. "You don't have a problem lying. Time has passed. We both agree Yasmin doesn't need to know what happened and we have no reason to tell her."

"You can handle lying to her every day?"

"As well as you. You got your way, friendship still intact. Now it's time for me to get her back."

"Oh, hell no. You chose to leave. I was fine keeping things between us before. I didn't interfere, I backed away. Your conscience got the best of you. Are you forgetting how you broke it off with her? She was still dealing with the death of your son and you told her a relationship was too much. Then you added salt to her wounds and said you wanted to see other people." I pause. "Do you really think you can go back, say I'm sorry and all is forgiven? Besides she is with Chauncey. I know you've seen the pictures and pictures don't lie. Chauncey is loving her lovely."

I knew that struck a nerve. The idea of Yasmin being with Chauncey hurt his pride. Looking at him I could see his mind spinning, wondering if Chauncey is a better boyfriend, no better lover. Now the selfish part coming in he can't accept that. Chauncey got the looks, the money, and his woman. Ego bruised. Mission accomplished.

I continue, "Yassy is a good girl, you know she deserves to be happy. She really had a hard time with the miscarriage..."

He cuts me off, "I know Landon, so did I!"

"Braxton calm down, I'm not saying you didn't. I'm just trying to get you to understand, Yasmin was devastated. She didn't know how to deal with things. You pushed her away when she needed you the most without any regard. Now she's with Chauncey, he puts a smile on her face. She's not hurting. You going back around will make her vulnerable. Open wounds that are not healed. It would be all bad."

Braxton walks away without responding. It was part truth.

Eric comes behind me and wraps his arms around me from behind startling me.

"You okay, sweetheart?"

"Yes," I say somewhat annoyed.

"What's wrong? I see you and Braxton were in a intense conversation."

"Yeah, he has the nerve to ask about Yassy. I told him to leave her alone. The way he broke up with her, now he wants to be concerned. She is happy with Chauncey."

"Yeah, Landon, but that's Yasmin decision to make."

I roll my eyes. She couldn't get back with him because of Eric and Javon.

It's been a rough couple of weeks. Braxton's ass had the audacity to approach me at the party asking if Eric was his son. Of course I denied it. Then he throws more insult asking who the father was because he damn sure knew Eric wasn't. I wanted to slap the shit out of him right there, but my environment wouldn't allow it. There would be payback. He didn't believe me, but he knew the possibility, if the truth came out. It would be disastrous. We both knew Eric's chances were slim to none. I lied and said Rocco. He shook his head. Fortunately, Yasmin was not in the picture or so I thought.

She devastated me when she told me she saw Braxton at the mall. Telling me all of these feelings came flooding back and how she wasn't over the jackass. Her happy-go-lucky ass is blinded and letting her heart dictate, not her brain. She's falling fast. I had to tell her he cheated. She sounded hurt and I thought she was ready to come into the light of common sense, but she started saying they both had issues and had to mature on some things. I swear I love Yassy, but my girl got that dopamine going on. Then again, thinking about the dick, yeah I understand. Braxton is an arrogant asshole, but his dick game will have you. His ass even had Melania's hoe ass hooked, and that trick has ran through the roster of the Ravens, Redskins, Wizards, climbing her way through the entire DMV, all up and down interstate 95. Yasmin's had her share of helpings of Braxton's dick, so she far gone. If I can convince her not to fuck him for a while and plant some tales, they'll both grow tired. But I better concentrate and handle my bigger problem… Rocco.

Weeks later, Melania was sitting in Braxton's lap, extra chunky. Her ass put on some weight. Nevertheless, I'd never been happier to see the hooker. I started to snap a picture to send to Yassy. He must be moving on. Yes, yes, yes. I knew reconciliation was done after Yas fucked Kevin. Yassy hadn't mentioned Braxton in months, life was good.

I answer my phone excitedly. Yassy had skipped town and didn't tell me. The nerve. I was anxious to find out all the details. I wanted to meet the mystery guy and thank him for getting rid of the butthole.

"Hey, Yassy!"

"Hey, my diva. I've missed you."

"I missed you too. How was your trip? Did you have a good time? Who did you go with?"

"Yes, I had a lovely time. Land, I have to tell you something?"

"What Yassy? You bought me back some La Perla?!" I sang.

"I did. Are you sitting?"

I'm cheesing hard, "Yes."

"I got married. Braxton surprised me, planned the whole thing."

Tears instantly ran down my face. I was fuming for so many reasons. "You did what? Yasmin, what were you thinking? You weren't supposed to take him back. Do you remember him breaking up with you? Oh my god, what did you do? Yasmin you can get it annulled."

"Whoa, Landon! You are really pissing me off. You're supposed to be happy for me."

"You were supposed to be my girl. You didn't tell me. I could have invited me to your wedding. You were at mine."

"It was a surprise."

"Whatever."

"Landon, stop being so damn dramatic. I want you to help us by a house."

"You have a house! Two, actually."

"We want a single-family."

"I'll get someone to show you some houses."

"Landon, you're that mad because you weren't there?"

"Yasmin, what do you want?"

"How about a congratulations."

"Congratulations." I force myself to say.

"Forget it, Landon. I'll use another realtor. What's the name and number?"

"I'll handle it."

"Bye, Landon." She hangs up before I could respond.

I sat for half-an-hour flabbergasted. I can't believe Yasmin's ass married Braxton. What the hell was she thinking? What the hell am I going to do? I just knew that relationship was done after Yassy had sex with

Kevin. Then again, I knew she was smart enough not to confess to that shit. I guess Melania's surgery was useless because it didn't lock that dick down. I called Kevin and spread the news. I knew Kevin and Yassy wouldn't work, but why he have to be an ass afterwards. I called to cuss him out.

"Kevin Powell."

"Kevin!" I practically screamed into the phone.

"Hello, Landon. What can I do for you?" he says sounding exasperated.

"You don't sound happy to hear from me."

He takes a deep breath, "Landon. I'm working on an important case. I don't have time to pacify you today."

"Fine. Just wanted you to know the love of your life married the ass. Goodbye!" I hung up the phone.

Within seconds the phone is ringing. I take my time answering.

"Hello, Kevin."

"Hold up. What happened?"

"Now you want to make time for me. As you say, you're ready to pacify me. Well I don't want the pacifier. I'm ready to go," I say annoyed.

"Landon, I apologize for hurting your feelings, but like I said, I was busy. I still stand by what I said. I am not pacifying and I'm not playing games. So are you going to tell me what's up or not?"

"Yasmin, went to the Islands and married Braxton," I cried.

"Damn, she did that?"

"I know. Why she do that? I know she wasn't thinking. Why'd she do something so stupid?" I cried.

"I know you don't like Braxton, but you don't have to cry."

"He's not good for her. He's going break her heart. He's still fucking around on her."

"Landon, what do you mean still fucking around? You knew this and didn't tell her?"

"No, I've seen him out with the same chick a few times."

"'Well, for Yas' sake, I hope he cut all ties."

"Damn Yassy. She didn't even invite me. I wish I knew because her ass wouldn't have made it in the dress or the damn plane."

"Landon, it's done. Support her. Be there if she need you."

"You know you're part to blame."

"Me?"

"Yeah you had to act like an ass after you got the goods. You could have been a gentleman had compassion, show good bedroom manner instead of, 'I got some ass. Get out!'"

"Landon, that's not how it went down. Furthermore…"

I cut him off, "Whatever Kevin you should have handled it better."

"Landon, what happened doesn't concern you, so I'm not discussing it with you."

"Whatever, Kevin! You were an ass. Why aren't you upset? What happened to all that emotion from earlier?"

"I was shocked, but when you think about it, it makes sense. No matter how you feel or want, Yasmin made her decision. You need to accept and respect that."

"This is why I can't talk to you. This righteous 'do the right thing' crap is for the birds."

"Landon, stop the theatrics."

"Kevin goodbye and this time don't call me back."

The phone rings again. I pick up the phone ready to tell Kevin off, "Didn't I tell you not to call me anymore."

"Who did you tell not to call you anymore?" Eric asked

Great, I wasn't feeling him right now either. Braxton being around more was going to be a problem. I put on my sweetest voice.

"I'm sorry, darling. I thought you were Kevin, he just pissed me off. I'm not dealing with him."

"Oh, so you're having another tantrum."

"I don't have tantrums."

"Ok, what do you call them meltdowns?"

"Eric, you about to be on my list next! What do you want?"

"Don't get mad because you ain't gettin' your way. What did Kevin do?"

"I told him Yasmin married that asshole Braxton."

He cuts me off excited. "Yassy and Braxton got married? That's good news!"

"No it isn't. It's horrible news. "

"Landon, get over it. That's what she wanted, support her. I told you, Braxton and Yasmin that's their relationship, their business. You can't run it or make her date who you want. I'm happy for them."

"Shut up! You sound like Kevin. Are you forgetting we just saw him out with Melania a few weeks ago? Me being happy for my friend when he was just with that hoe? I won't be doing that."

"Well Landon, it's a done deal. Anyway, back to what I was calling you about. I'm going to take Eric to visit my aunt and Nana."

"Ok, love you."

"Love you too, sweetheart."

I locked myself in the office and cried. I prayed my Yassy wouldn't get hurt again. But I cried and prayed even more that little Eric was somehow big Eric's son and my sexual encounter with Braxton never got out.

17

It Don't Mean A Thing

At the last minute, I decided to attend a listening party for an R&B singer by the name of Dejuan. Braxton, his friend Cory, and his brother Vincent were posted at the bar when I walked in. Perfect, I needed to straighten some things out with Braxton.

"Braxton, I need to have a talk with you."

"I'm busy." His attention goes back to Cory's conversation with Vincent.

"Hello, Landon," Corey and Vincent greet me.

"Sorry, hello to both of you. Braxton, I'm about two seconds from going off on you. Do you really want me to?"

"Do you think you can come over here threaten me and think I would follow you because you said so?"

"I figured you would want to hear what I have to say."

"Why would I do that? Never mind, come on." We walked to the corner. He wastes no time getting straight to the point. "What do you want?"

"Well I guess it's a good sign you're wearing your wedding ring," I say cynically.

"This is what you wanted to talk to me about?"

"Yes! Why the hell did you marry Yassy?"

"The reason people get married."

"Your relationship isn't right."

"My relationship with Yasmin is mine, not yours. Stay out of it."

"Braxton, you just don't know how much I want to hit you right now," I grunted.

"Don't tell me you caught feelings."

"Oh, hell no! You don't have enough money for me and you act too much like a punk ass. So not my type. I don't do controlling wannabe pimps. That catastrophe that happened between us was just that. My concern is Yasmin."

"Like I said, my MARRIAGE, my business."

"Not when you marry my friend and are still fucking that hoe Melania. I will tell Yasmin and your marriage will get annulled. Daddy and Kevin can erase it from the books like that," I snap my finger.

I turn to walk away, he grabs my arm. "Hold the fuck up! You ain't gon' do shit. Don't you even think about bothering or upsetting my wife. Your problem is you all worried about my shit, worry about yours. I told you before where I stand as far as Yasmin. All that shit is in the past. I haven't fucked around with Melania in a minute or anyone. I am committed to Yasmin. Despite what you think, I do love her." He pauses, releases my arm. "Now you listen to me. You will respect my relationship. Don't call my WIFE putting this bullshit in her ear. Do you understand? Control that mouth of yours. I'm not Eric you are not going to boss me around."

"I apologize, but if you hurt her, I swear I will have you fucked up."

"Landon, don't threaten me. Didn't I just tell you I'm not for your bullshit? Shut up for once. We can both agree we love Yasmin. I'm not trying to or plan to hurt her. I know the same goes for you. So don't interfere in our relationship and I won't interfere in yours. You got that?"

"Yes, Braxton," I give him a phony smile.

Here I was again trying to be nice sitting at one these boring basketball games. I really was trying to show Eric support. Eric and I lead separate lives. For our son's sake, I was trying to be a family unit. Little Eric adored him and he the same. Truth be told, I was a little jealous. Every day, I made it a point to spend the morning with little Eric. We'd have breakfast, watch TV, and attend Mommy and me classes twice a week. He was my priority. At night I did hang out, maybe a little too much. I was jealous of Big Eric because due to his schedule, he had less time, but in every activity, he wanted his daddy, that father-son bond.

"Hey, Landon."

Tonya, Thomas Duke's wife says. Tommy and Eric were both Wizards. Tonya was pretty plain. Meaning she was not a natural beauty, make-up improved her appearance. The term "beautiful liar" was created with her in mind. Judging from the acne breaking through her make-up, if the make-up was removed, I'd see blotched, scaly skin. I bet her caramel complexion wasn't authentic either looking at her hands, which were two shades darker. Don't know what she had over Thomas to convince him to marry her. Scanning her attire, I see. Like her, it was plain. Her outfit bought off a bargain rack at a local store such as Target. Tonight she wore a pair of jeans that did nothing to enhance her derriere. The blue and white Washington Wizards t-shirt she wore came from one of the vendors. She finished her outfit with plain two-inch boots. With her, he didn't have to worry about going broke, which was a good thing since he spent over $100,000 grand each month coming to parties. With so much wrong, she had the audacity to be an instigator. Knew everybody business but her own, but at least her short weave looked good.

"Hey," I respond with my fakest smile.

"I haven't seen you in while. I was wondering what was up."

"I've been working. You know I have my own real estate company. Right now, I'm offering home buying classes."

"Oh, so business is doing well."

"Business is doing excellent."

"I heard Thomas mention your course."

I had to smirk. At every party, he selected the gold package.

"Girl, you need to start coming to these games. These groupies been after your honey. You know I got your back though. Ain't nothin' happenin' on my watch."

"Girl, I ain't worried about that, but thanks for having my back."

"Yeah girl, anytime. You know these players. We lucky our men know how to keep their dick in their pants."

She puts her hand up for a high five.

I wasn't cosigning with her cluelessness. I give her a wave. "Girl, you crazy." If you only knew. Shit, her man bought me my new Birkin bag.

Tonya rambles non-stop throughout the game, bragging, giddy over her new car. It's a starter car, a BMW1 series. Conversation like this with these phony chicks who tried too hard irritated me. It was too fake and I liked my privacy. I could only watch these players run up and down the court so many times. Thank God for modern technology. I pulled out my cell, took a selfie, and played a computer game, ending up running my battery low. Fortunately, there were only 15 minutes left. I was yawning when I heard Tonya mention Melania.

"So her son is a cutie."

"What Melania's ass had a baby? I am out of the loop. When?"

"A while ago. Two years. From what I've seen, the baby busted her up. She lost the body."

"What? I haven't seen her in a while." In truth, I rarely saw her. Other than months ago with Braxton, when she was noticeably heavier. The girls she recruited were still top-notch though. I knew she kept them together. I didn't miss her absence though because she had her clone, Ty, there to annoy me, sometimes even more than she did.

"Girl, yes. She had a baby by Chris Young."

"Chris Young? I'm convinced she on drugs. Ain't no sane, blind, or common sense individual gonna have a baby by him. He got what, 12 kids?"

Tonya laughed. "I know, right?"

"Ten baby mamas too? Well, 11 now. Her stock is in the negative for real. I expected better from her."

"That caught me off guard too," she cosigned.

"That hooker is smoking or sniffing something. I can't believe she was that stupid. Say no to drugs."

"Stop it Landon, she ain't on drugs. Then again Chris is nasty. I don't believe he knows a shower."

"Just when I think she can't get any more trifling she proves me wrong. I see her ass must be loving that nose candy."

Tonya shakes her head.

18

Pressure

"Mommy, why didn't you tell me Yasmin and I were sisters? I expect Daddy to lie, not you!"

I confronted Mommy in her downtown Silver Spring office. At Yasmin and Braxton's housewarming the big secret was revealed, Yasmin and I are sisters. Daddy and Yasmin's mother Michelle had a brief affair. Yasmin was the result. Daddy and Michelle agreed that Michelle's husband John would raise Yasmin as his own. Daddy provided financial support.

"Landon, please."

"Mommy, why did you lie?!"

"I told you, you are the best. Playing second or competing with anyone was never an option for you. All the attention was on you. No need to share. Can you imagine what life would have been like?"

"Mommy, I wanted a sister. You should have said something."

"You grew close anyway. So in essence you got your wish. If you grew up together sharing or fighting for your father's time, it would have caused resentment. I know. You see you don't know your aunts."

"Mommy, you don't know that."

"When I grew up, I was the oldest. I was responsible for making sure my bratty sisters did what they had to do. Stuck babysitting. It was harder for me. I was expected to set the example, behave correctly. I spent my time babysitting, cleaning. I missed out on a lot of my childhood. If they messed up, I was in trouble. It never mattered that they didn't listen to me. When I graduated and became a lawyer as daddy wanted, they couldn't hide their resentment. I saved you. Trust me, having siblings is overrated."

I sigh.

"So say you're welcome and be more appreciative."

"Yes, mommy," I concede.

She rambles, "Even after I accomplished what they wanted, my parents still expected me to help my siblings out financially, help them with jobs. Absolutely not! They didn't make it easy on me. They were given even more opportunities. My parents spoiled them and they are responsible for dealing with the consequences." She pauses. "Landon, my baby I made sure you had opportunities. I also instilled in you ambition, strength, tenacity. You know you are the best. You are very successful, you have a handsome husband that is a multi-millionaire. I am so proud. What I did was best."

"Do I have any other siblings?"

"None."

Mommy when she started coming to the house you should have told me. Especially since Yasmin's mother treated her so badly."

"You're my child; my interest was and still is you."

"It still doesn't make it right."

"Your father provided money. It's not my fault her slut of a mother used it for her personal gain."

"That is true."

"Landon, don't dwell on this. You have the sister

you always wanted. Enough of the past. Focus on your family and security. I must say your husband adores you. You're doing everything perfectly." She smiles.

If only she knew.

Eric's putting this pressure on me, I can't fall for him. It's hard because Eric is so affectionate. It's overwhelming, yet comforting with everything going on. I have to resist temptation. Men and security do not go hand-in-hand. The revelation of Yasmin paternity is reinforcement as to why I can't get any more emotionally tied to Eric. Besides, Eric is a professional basketball player. Groupies are like ants, everywhere. His ass has wandered. Be smart, Landon. Braxton loves Yasmin yet his dick found its ways in me and Melania. Like Mommy said, reap the benefits.

One thing I learned mutually from my parents, the importance of research. I didn't abide by that old saying, don't go looking for trouble. I looked at it as gathering info, preparing my case. Guilty until proven innocent. In my office, I did an internet search on Eric. Checking the entertainment blogs was so tedious. I know a lot of them were fictitious. Pictures are what I wanted. To his credit, there wasn't much out there. I ran across more pictures of me at various events.

Oh look and you shall find. On the screen was a picture of Eric with a Kim Kardashian clone. It was the same chick I had words with in L.A. Weeks ago Eric, Braxton, Yassy and I flew out for the BET awards. Nicollette was her name. She stood ready and willing to jump on Eric's dick. In actuality, she was literally on his dick, sitting in his lap and him with a big Kool-Aid smile. I thought I shut it down, but obviously I didn't. Again proving men ain't shit! See, this is why I didn't invest my heart. My advantage, my man is wealthy. Landon is about to do her after this utter disrespect. Since Eric showed his ass mine was off limits.

Normally, I avoided the sex parties, tonight I needed to unwind, relieve some tension. As mommy says, make him pay. As usual, the party was live and even more scandalous than before. Every corner some type of sex act was being performed. Women with strap-ons penetrating men and women in bondage, they were beyond my limits. I drew the line at penetrating men. Nonetheless, different strokes for different folks. Their fetishes inflated my pockets, so carry-on.

Surprisingly, I found a secluded spot next to the bar. Taking a seat on the stool, I allowed my body to groove with the music. The DJ played Rick Ross's Aston Martin Music.

Thomas, Tonya's husband, eased his way in front of me.

"What's going on with you?"

"You tell me," I flirt.

"Looks like you have everything going on." He uses his hands to spread my thighs, stepping right in between. His hands roam up my skirt, around my hips.

I should have brushed him away, but my vendetta against his wife allowed him the privilege. The gossip queen saw me with Javon and Rocco. She painted the picture that things were very intimate, prompting Eric to ask the extent of our business. He knew I was the agent they used to rent the mansions, but he didn't know I received a percentage. She further insinuated that she'd seen me around town a lot. Which now that I think about it was probably the reason Eric had Nicollete in his lap. None of these chicks could be trusted. Instead of running her mouth, she should be keeping her mouth on her husband's dick.

"Looks like you need some tension relief."

"I do."

"Judging from last week's game, I think you need some practice. You lost the ball a few times. Your aim was off too."

"Oh, you got jokes."

He rotates his hip, grind into me. Through his clothes I knew he had a nice size package.

"Are you enjoying the party?"

"I am now."

Thomas and I continued to touch each other. Through clothes I massaged his tool; he massaged my breast, clit. He didn't flinch when I came, just grinded harder. On the dance floor he had me in an embrace, hot breath on my neck and collar bone, turning me on.

The party lacked privacy, I opted to follow Thomas to an after-hours spot. The place was dark, exotic, smell of weed filled the room. It wasn't my elite type of establishment. He leads up to a plush sofa located behind a curtained door. He orders drinks before he takes a seat.

He attempts to kiss my lips, I swerve away, "You can't kiss these lips, but you can kiss these."

I spread my legs. Thomas wastes no time diving in. He's rough. I have to remind him he is kissing a jewel, appreciate. With many drinks and instructions, he finally gets it.

"Lick, lick, lick, lick, the clit. Suck gentle, a little more pressure. Now lick, lick. Stick your tongue in me, Thomas, lick lick, suck. That's it. Fuck me with your tongue. Drink up all that honey. Get it."

Thomas was an exceptional student, a quick study. As a result, I gave him a hand job. My only complaint, Thomas moaned like a girl attracting a lot of attention. Bystanders observed. I won't lie, the effects of smoke-filled ambiance had me enjoying the center of attention. I literally saw quite a few men, females mouths salivate. Thomas' tongue had been drinking me up so long, my legs were numb. I had lost track of the amount of orgasms long ago. Delirious, ready for penetration, I pushed Thomas head away. Ever so anxious, he attempted to slide in me. I halted his attempt, grabbing a condom from the table. Reluctantly he puts it on. He slides in, does it real slow. In this area, he needs no instruction. He fucked me long, hard, just as I needed. Long, sensual, deep, heightening my orgasm while lengthening at the same time. Feeling so good, I allowed a stranger to suck on my nipples. I return the favor giving him a hand job.

Thomas is about to come, I can't tell his breathing more labored, I take my free hand to reach for Thomas balls. I massage them, which causes him to whimper. My intruder almost at his climax sucking my nipples harder than before, sending an electrifying surge throughout my body. I explode as I feel Thomas go limp and the intruder squirts.

"Damn, better than I thought," he pants.

We dress, opting to lie limply upon each other to catch our breath, restore some energy. Unintentionally, I doze off. I'm not sure how many minutes passed before I felt him move my hips down the sofa to get another taste. I do remember more drinks, more bystanders, and a lot more orgasms.

The next morning, I work up in the Marriot naked. No sign of Thomas.

19

Trouble

I don't know what the fuck happened, who did it. He drugged me, had to. Quickly I dressed and went home to be greeted by a furious Eric.

Over the weeks, our relationship had drastically changed. We barely talk. My all-nighter had the relationship in the coffin, ready to be buried. I knew the only reason he tolerated me was because of the baby.

Not fucking again. I was on my knees leaning over the toilet. It wasn't even noon and I had thrown up five times. I knew I was pregnant. Just like before, I didn't know who the father was. I couldn't go through another eight months hoping Eric was the father. It's hard enough watching him bond with him knowing there was no biological connection. I couldn't take the risk of having another child that wasn't his. I don't remember anything from that night. I knew someone slipped something in my drink. What they did, how many guys violated me, I didn't know. I knew then though that I had to get an abortion this time.

I sat numb as the doctor went over my results, "If you go through with this the chances of you conceiving again are less than one percent. As you know, the culture revealed you contracted syphilis, gonorrhea and chlamydia."

'*What the fuck?!*' *is* all I remember saying. It could have been worse. I could have herpes or HIV. The only good thing was, I haven't fucked Eric since my indiscretions with other guys.

I wanted to cry, but anyone seeing me weak, or being weak, was not an option. Having this baby was not an option. I couldn't pen another kid on Eric or walk around with the guilt like I have been. I terminated the pregnancy. I would have given Eric a baby, but after my night, all the sexually transmitted diseases, and last abortion, the chances of me conceiving are not likely. Partying became my way of life. Home only reminded me of what I had lost, the abortion constantly haunting me.

As an athlete's wife, I was often invited to charity events, for the most part they were boring. But it was better than being home. Tonight was no different until I spotted Melania in the corner trying to be discreet. I hate to admit her white Max Azria pantsuit was cute. She's been in the gym, her body more voluptuous than before. But even still, I taunt.

"Melania, no date tonight?"

"Landon, I'm not in the mood today."

I ignore her, "I heard you got your shit tightened and you still can't keep a man. Yep, Braxton got married. Cory moved on. You should ask the doctor for a refund."

"Landon, you're still jealous. You wake up thinking about my Jayjay. Listening to you, you know where it's been. Who's seen it. All this inquiring you must want a taste. Sorry, I don't do girls. If you're good, I may throw you my panties."

"Nobody is jealous of you. What do you have?"

"Obviously, something you like. Every time you see me you make it a point to come sniffing, I told you no licking. If you're a good girl, I may break my rules. You being the giver."

"Ha, nobody wants your ass. Braxton didn't want that processed worn out vajayjay. Like with Paul, jokes on you. Gave it up to the wrong one again.

"I could be like you and let a good one slip away. Eric is tipping." She laughs.

Rocco came in. I swear I saw Melania go from looking stressed to being scared.

I had to ask. "Are you okay?"

"Yes," but her hands were trembling.

"What's up with you and Rocco?"

She pays no attention to me. Instead, looks like she goes deep in thought. She pops a pill like candy.

Minutes later, "You ever get tired?"

"What do you mean?" I ask curiously.

"Landon, we don't like each other, but I will give you some advice, be careful of Rocco. Don't get in too deep.

"What are you talking about? No trivial pursuit or guessing games."

"If you can, walk away."

"So you can get all the money?"

"It's much deeper than that..Forget it. Just be careful." She walks away.

20

Hurt Me Soul

I sat on the chaise longue in my massive closet trying to select an outfit for tonight. BET was having a screening party for a new scripted TV series they were debuting. I sat there carefree, not realizing the domino effects of my life were about to take place. One fall after another, quick, and too fast. No way to change the course, the only thing left, to see how they fall.

"Landon. I've had enough of your shit. I'm done."

"What are you talking about, Eric?"

"Your days of talking to me any kind of way are over. I filed for divorce this morning."

"What?" Panic, Eric's leaving me? No. I don't get left. I don't get hurt. My stomach twists in a ball of knots.

"You heard me. I'm tired of your disrespect. Talking to me like I'm your child. I tried with you."

"I tried with you. You tried to make me a housewife. You knew from day one that ain't me. You tried to mold me into someone I'm not."

"All I asked you for was support. I asked you to come to games, support me. Your problem is you're spoiled. You have your father jumping through hoops trying to please your ass. Your mother pumping up your conceited ass. You think everybody supposed to be at your beckon call."

"That is not true. You are confusing that with confidence. I am strong-willed. I am a queen, so I expect the best. What's wrong with that? You should be honored to have me as your wife. You are envied by many."

"Listen to yourself. I told you I'm leaving you. You don't try to stop me, tell me you love me or let's try to work this out. No, you holler I should be honored.I'm done with this." He holds his hand up in surrender.

As much as I did want him to stay, I don't beg. I don't cry. "Eric, I'm sorry you feel that way."

"I don't believe your ass is so shallow."

I don't believe his ass is leaving me. I'm not good at being sensitive. It's not in my nature, I don't know how to pacify him. This is a new obstacle for me. I'm sure my face reads confusion.

"I'm taking little Eric with me. We will work out some custody arrangement."

"You're not taking my son anywhere."

"Your son?" He gives me a quizzical looks that renders me speechless.

Damn, he got me all fucked up today. I recover. "Our son is staying with me."

"From the looks of things, you were on your way out. You weren't watching anybody kids, meaning your own. You look like you're trying to reclaim that single life. I'm just helping you out."

"Eric just because I'm going out doesn't mean I'm trying to be single or neglect my parental responsibilities. I'm just going out for a little me time."

"Exactly, it's always about Landon."

"That's not true, darling."

"Cut that darling crap. Okay Landon, what is it about? You say it's not about you. Tell me why the hell you had an abortion."

Oh no, not that. Breathe. Get it together, Landon. "We are at a bad place. I didn't want to bring another innocent person into our arguing."

"That's how you justify killing our child. You don't think I should have been involved in that decision?"

"You would have talked me into having the baby."

"And what was so wrong with that?"

I don't say anything.

"You don't have an answer."

"I honestly wish I didn't do it. We can try to have another baby." I will not cry. Damn, why did I go out that night?

"You can't just replace a baby, Landon. That baby was innocent. Don't I take care of Eric? From day one was there making bottles, changing diapers, getting up in the middle of the night. Did I ever complain? You didn't have to do shit."

He was so right. "You're right. I am sorry," I say sincerely.

"I am too, Landon. I moved most off my stuff out this afternoon while you were shopping. I will get the other stuff later."

I survey the room for the first time. Our adjoining closet walk-in suite had a substantial amount of his clothes that were missing. He bamboozled my ass.

"Landon, go ahead, go out. Enjoy. I will take Eric. I'll bring him back tomorrow night. We can sit down to discuss a custody agreement."

Being as nonchalant as I could, I say, "Fine Eric."

Back to my scheduled program, I thought. I think I feel like the color red tonight. Picking out a red Herve'

Leger Novelty cocktail dress and silver Christian
Louboutin silver spiked pumps, I was ready to do what
Eric said, go out. And I did, however I didn't enjoy it.

Weeks after Eric left me, he hit me with a demoral-
izing blow. I knew it in my heart, but hearing him say
it, I was like one of the theatrical guests on the Maury
Povich show falling to my knees. *God no!* Eric stood
with a mixture of rage and hurt. His hurt overpowering
his rage, tears flowed freely from his eyes. His cries,
"No, he my son. My son, he my son. Why?"

He asked me who the father was and I lied saying it
was a one-night stand. I wouldn't admit to Braxton ever.
If I had my way, Eric would never find out Lil' Eric's
paternity.

The night Braxton dropped Eric off from his parent's
cookout, I told him about Eric's results. He didn't take
the news well. He kept whining saying I should have
told him the truth when I first found out I was pregnant,
especially after he was born. He yapped on and on giving me a migraine. At first I was going to take it to my
grave, I hated to hurt my sister. I wasn't going to involve
Braxton in any way. Then I thought, what if my son had
a medical emergency. Reliving the fiasco with Yasmin, I
didn't want my son to grow up thinking his father didn't
want to be bothered with him. I didn't want my baby
having self-esteem issues like Yassy. We agreed to get
the test done as soon as possible. He was praying the test
would reveal Rocco as the father. Little did he know, I
never had sex with Rocco during that time.

I walk into my bedroom to Eric reading the paternity papers confirming Braxton as little Eric's father. Oh
damn, the walls were closing in. How can I rationalize
this to him?

He comes rushing towards me and slaps me across
the room, catching me completely off guard.

"You been fucking Braxton?"

"Just once."

"Who else?"

I knew never to admit even when caught, "No one."

"Landon, I am through with your bullshit. Who else have you been fucking?"

"That's it."

"Check your phone."

He forwards a text of me having sex with Thomas.

That motherfucker. I was going to get his ass.

"You still want to play games?"

"No, that was before we were married." I lied.

"Your ass still wants to lie to me, bitch!" Eric slapped me as the nanny was coming in with little Eric. Little Eric runs up trying to secure me. Crying daddy NO!

The maid quickly took little Eric out of the room, kicking and screaming.

Eric's eyes followed little Eric and I saw the streams falling from his eyes. My heart stopped. Damn, I could see him mentally breaking down in front of me. I wanted to reach out, apologize, tell him, how sorry I really was. I never wanted it to be like this, but I knew better. His eyes focused on the door where the only son he knew had just left. Eric cries. I could see it ripping at his heart. His leaving signifying the son he knew was gone.

Eric head dropped, I could see his six foot eight frame wobble. His legs looked weak as if they were ready to collapse. He took in deep breaths wobbling as he walked to the door leaving. Soon after, I heard the front door close and I slid to the floor.

21

Leave Me Alone

"Landon, what were you thinking? How the hell you get pregnant by your sister's husband," my father berates.

Daddy had me inside of his home office lecturing me about the catastrophe with Braxton. Really, I mean, really. I was trying not to let my temper get the best of me and go off on daddy. He was pushing every button.

"At the time they weren't married and I didn't know she was my sister, daddy. Remember you didn't tell me."

He's mad, continuing, "You were out of line!"

"I guess you can say like father like daughter. Déjà vu. At least I admitted my indiscretion."

"Landon, I am your father. Watch your mouth, little girl."

"Well what do you want me to say? Just like you, I fucked up. I'm sorry. You think what you're saying I haven't heard or said to myself. Maybe I inherited the cheating gene from you. How long did it take you to get your stuff in order? Or did you? I've seen you enough. Very sloppy daddy, especially since you are a lawyer."

"Landon, watch your damn mouth I am your father. I've had enough of your disrespect. Talk to me like you got some sense. Little girl get that attitude of yours in check now!" He voice boisterous.

"Well cut the self-righteous act! You told me a long time ago don't trust men. You've proven I should take heed. Perhaps you should have been a daddy to Yasmin also and gave her that valuable lesson."

"Landon."

"Daddy."

"Landon, I know I haven't been the best example but I hoped you would have known better. Known boundaries."

"Do you think I really went out there to hurt Yasmin or have a baby by Braxton? You don't know me obviously. What is done is done. I can't change it. I know it was wrong. I really do regret it, but what do you want me to do? Your lecture heard, done, over it, next. To my credit, I did come forward. I didn't wait twenty plus years."

"What are you planning to do?"

"Daddy, really. Are you lecturing me? I don't know. What do you suggest? Then again, why would I take advice from you? You still don't have your stuff in order. Why don't you lead by example?"

Before he could respond, I walked out of the house making sure I slammed the door behind me.

Yasmin had been missing for over a month. I pray every day that she comes home, even if she doesn't talk to me, I just need to know she is okay. This is the worst feeling of having no one to talk to, to vent, to laugh, and Kevin is a horrible substitute. He invited me over to his place for dinner. His plain, sneaky girlfriend Nicole wasn't there, thankfully.

"Landon, what were you thinking?"

"Kevin, I'm not the only one to fuck up."

"I know, but it's still shocking. Damn, Braxton got both of y'all knocked up. The irony."

"Kevin!"

"I know, I'm just like damn."

"Just get it all out. I'm tired of everyone and these damn questions! It happened! We both were drunk. No, I didn't want Braxton. No, I still don't want his ass. I can't stand the punk. I know I was wrong, but I can't erase that catastrophe. Anything else?"

"Why didn't you say anything before?"

"How do you tell your best friend you got drunk and fucked her man while she was grieving over a miscarriage?"

"So you were going to take it to your grave?"

"Yes, and I thought Eric was the father."

"I know DNA is crazy and all, but you've seen Eric's black ass. Your baby doesn't have one feature that could possibly or remotely belong to Eric."

I throw my fork at Kevin.

"I'm just saying."

"Kevin!"

"Did you and Braxton hook up after they broke up?"

"Hell no!"

"So Braxton never knew he could be the daddy? You never told him? Not even when he and Yasmin got back together? That's why you reacted the way you did when they got married. In retrospect, don't you think you should have said something beforehand?"

"Enough with this cross examining. I am not on the stand and I will go in contempt and slap your ass." This is the reason I only deal with Kevin in spurts. Yassy said it best, he needs to be a friend not a lawyer. *God, please let Yassy be ok.*

"Do you have any idea where Yassy is?"

"No," Kevin said shaking his head.

"I really fucked up. What do you think I should do?"

"Right now you have to give her some space. She's been hurt by her sister and her husband. She's not in the right frame of mind. She has a lot to deal with. Don't push."

"Tell her I'm sorry if you talk to her."

"Landon, that won't do anything. She's not ready to hear that."

22

My Apology

My prayers had been answered. Yasmin's ass came home pregnant, with twins no less. She wasn't dealing with my ass, which hurt. More importantly though, she was safe. I had no one to talk to. My mommy had a big case, so she was busy. Talking to Kevin was a chore. All he knew how to do was lecture and cross examine, so annoying. Indulging more into night life, I literally tried to dance and drink my pain away. The parties with Javon and Rocco were still lucrative so that aspect of my life was wonderful. I rewarded myself with a bronze colored Aston Martin DB9. Bored out my mind, I sat at the Fire and Ice after hour hookah lounge.

While I was taking a break at the bar, I saw Cory and Javon. Then I spot Vincent and Braxton. Damn, I definitely don't feel like this evil motherfucker. Vincent was talking, but I could tell Braxton wasn't paying attention. He had an expression as though he was mad at the world. I wanted to ignore them both, but Braxton's evil ass looks up and sees me. He signals for me to come over. I raise eyebrows letting him know he had to bring his evil ass to me, and then put the hand on hip for emphasis.

Vincent approaches me with him. I don't care. For the most part, we're still cordial.

Getting right to the point, "What do you want?"

"What happened at your father's house with Yasmin?"

A few days ago, Yasmin went to my parents' house. Daddy, still going with the façade of father of the year, tried to make amends. I confessed to Yasmin that Braxton was remorseful over our incident. I even admitted I could have stopped it. I know, stupid.

"How do you know about that?"

"I overheard her talking to Kevin," he grunts.

I laugh. "You really are pathetic. Eavesdropping, really?"

"You really are a bitch."

"Such a harsh thing to say about your son's mother," I scowl.

Vincent steps in, "Braxton, you were wrong."

He stares at Vincent, eventually he does apologize.

"I told you we had to tell her gradually. You had to do it your way."

"Braxton I don't care if we told her in front of a priest, the pope, a judge, mother Theresa or a room full of people, either way, she would have acted the same."

He takes a breath and said. "What happened?"

He may have apologized, but I wasn't over his remark. "I told her what really went down that night. How I rode your anaconda, how you loved it and was BEGGING for more."

Vincent taken aback, but knew to restrain Braxton. I don't flinch. I wait a few seconds before I tell the truth, well almost the whole truth.

"Why are you so damn evil?"

"I told her it was a mistake. Told her you and I were drunk. Us hooking up was never intentional. I even told her how bad you felt afterwards. I made sure I told her it was the only one time." I purposely omitted the part where I admitted to her I could have stopped it. His crazy ass would definitely kirk out.

"Good."

"So you should be thanking me."

"Thanking you?"

"Yes, I took the blame. I told her you wanted to tell her the truth, but I convinced you not to."

"Are you forgetting you told me not to say anything? Shit, has my wife forgiven me? Is she talking to me? No! She's two seconds from divorcing my ass. So your confession ain't do shit."

"I could have said a lot more because I know you enjoyed every bit of it. Like I said, you should be thanking me."

"I can't stand your ass."

"The feeling is mutual. I can't believe my ass was drunk enough to allow you this privilege."

"Landon you are a hoe! Many were given that privilege."

"And so are you, let's not go there. Does Yassy know you hang around pimps and sample their products? Melania, in particular? Oh slutty Melania! You went there and try to call me a hoe. My dear sister doesn't know everything, does she?"

Braxton stares me down and I stare back just as hard.

"Last I heard, Melania is still pissed off about your last encounter and that little mishap. Yeah, you thought I didn't know. I know a lot. That's why I didn't want Yassy with your controlling ass."

Melania caught feelings. Let's just say, like me, she was not pleased about their marriage. Heard she threatened to call Yassy to give her an earful. Braxton grabbed her ass. My sources say he didn't physically harm her. One has to wonder though what would have happened if there weren't any witnesses.

"I'm bored with you and I have better things to do. I will leave you with this. I won't be too many more of your hoes or bitches. Your past is just as scandalous as mine, even more. Javon, Cory, the stories I could tell, but I won't for now. So show me some respect."

23

Bad Habbit

"Damn, Javon. Damn, damn! Oh shit!"

"That's it." He removes his head from between my thighs.

"Your tongue is your best asset."

"No, Mr. Wonderful is."

"Nah, he average." Which it was average length average girth, just like his game average.

"Turn over let me get some of that ass. I'll really make that ass scream."

"Maybe later. What did you want to talk to me about?"

Javon had just finished relieving my tension. We were lying in his round, custom made, gel foam bed. After the party last night, I opted to stay with him at his condo instead of driving the thirty minutes home.

I figured I'd mention the escorts from the previous evening. "Some of the girls last night looked like top-model rejects,"

"I know, Ty was in charge last night. She showed she didn't know what the fuck she was doing."

"Why didn't Melania handle it? I know there were a lot of complaints. If I paid $50,000 for a platinum package I would demand a refund."

"Melania has decided to take a leave of absence."

"Old girl can't hang. People stopped paying $20,000 for that worn out trap."

"Why, are you going to take her place?"

I slap Javon in the head. "I am not a hoe. This jewel is not for sale or rent."

"Yeah, yeah, that's what you all say. At least Melania never denied it. She knew the game. Get that money and next."

"Don't compare me to that hooker."

"You still salty from Paul years ago. Girl, you petty."

"It's about principle. I went to that trick like a lady, yet she still chose to disrespect me."

"That was your first mistake. You know it's no honor in hoes. The object is get that money. Later for the respect shit you yappin'. You get it while you can before the next bitch come along. Respect the hustle."

I give him a scowl.

"Landon, get over it."

"Javon, why are things always tit for tat with you?"

"It's life. He wanted what Melania was offering. If he didn't, he could have said no. In this industry, chances are we gonna fuck the same girl, you gonna fuck the same dude at some point. No need to become territorial."

"Is that what you told Braxton?"

"Braxton acting like a bitch ass."

"What you expect? You were trying to fuck his wife," I sang.

"But I didn't. She said no."

"But you tried and if you could…."

He laughs. "Most def, I know it gots to be good. Chauncey even slowed it down when he was fucking Yasmin. Point is, I didn't."

I shake my head, "It's about principle."

"He's fucked chicks I fucked."

"Which none of whom you were in a relationship with or even thought about getting serious with. You know what, why am I even wasting time with ya ass? You don't get it. You have no morals. "

"Says the chick who has a baby by the husband."

Disregarding his hurtful remark, "What do you want to do about Melania, Javon?"

"Since business is doing so well, I think we should expand.

"Have you discussed this with Rocco?"

Ignoring me, he continues. "Since Melania is on leave indefinitely, we were thinking you should start your own modeling agency."

Ironically, I like the idea, but I wanted it to be legit my way.

He continues, "We can recruit girls. They would be used in music videos, promotions, our parties. You would screen them. Make sure we don't have a repeat of last night."

"Sounds like a plan."

Something told me Javon and Rocco were in too deep. I know I agreed to expand due to Melania's absence, but I decided to go another route. Instinct told me there was a lot of other shit going on at those parties. From the constant bad vibes, I knew I had to branch out, do my own thing, especially after the incident with one of the models being brutally attacked. Business with them did provide a lot of contacts. Some clients essentially came to me to purchase homes. I did collect some nice commission checks. However, I became addicted to that fast money. Real estate is cool, but it was too much paperwork and work at times. I started an image consultant firm, which included my two favorite hobbies: shopping and spending other people's money. I styled many of my male admirers. I even helped the lost groupies convert their image like Melissa Forte. The commission from that hustle was profitable, but not like the parties. I had to do something else to quickly dissolve my business dealings with Javon and Rocco soon.

Rocco strolls into my office without a knock or invitation. He closes the door before taking a seat. Rocco normally a stylish dresser bypassed his normal suit and tie attire. Today he looked like a thug, dark blue religion jeans, black fitted shirt, fitted hoodie over his shirt with black steel toe boots.

"Hello, Rocco. Next time a call or some courtesy would be appreciated before you decide to just come into my office."

"How's business?"

"You know business is well, Rocco."

"I'm talking about your side hustle."

"Oh, that's doing fine."

"Really?"

"Yes, how are you, Rocco?"

"Where's my cut?"

"The money from the parties is in the account."

"I'm referring to money you made from your hustle."

"Do I ask you for a percentage from your other businesses?"

"I want 40 percent."

"Rocco, that is my money. We agreed money made from the party was split. Other business ventures were not included in that agreement."

"Not when it is affecting my business. Not when your business is based off of my contacts."

"Rocco, it doesn't matter. Your parties are successful because you have access to my tax id. We're even. You have a legitimate business to clean your money. That's the extent of our business relationship. What ventures I do outside of our parties are mine," I say sternly.

"Is that so?"

"Yes. If you can't respect that, then we need to end all business ties." I take a sip from my glass of water.

"You're threatening me?" He smirks.

"No, not at all. I'm just stating the facts. You need me. Therefore, the money I make outside of the parties is mine."

Rocco has an intense glare. I don't flinch.

"Agreed? Do you understand?"

Rocco doesn't respond. He gets up and leaves out of the door.

Later that evening, I arrived at the party to check out the few girls I recruited when I was overseeing the modeling agency. I went into one of the bedrooms of the mansion. Asia, one of the models I interviewed was at the mirror brushing her hair. When I stood behind her, reflection in the mirror, she never acknowledged me.

Asia seemed aloof.

I snapped my fingers, "Asia, are you ok?"

She jumps. The crazed look in her eyes alarmed me.

"Asia, maybe you need to go home. I don't think you're up for this."

Frantically, she begins shaking her head. "I'm fine. Ready for work."

Despite being in a sedated state, her outfit was a cute, black spandex shirt with tights in thigh-high boots and sheer white button up blouse.

"I don't think so."

She takes a blue pill from the dresser, popping it in her mouth. "I'll be good in a few minutes."

"Asia, what the hell did you just take? We have a 'no drug' policy." I was flabbergasted. She wasn't the girl from a month ago. The girl I hired was vibrant, alert, actually my favorite, by far the prettiest. Her high-cheek-bones, full lips and almond shaped eyes still called for attention. Now, her eyes were vacant, her mocha skin dull, she was like a zombie.

"Asia, why are you taking drugs?"

I'm not naïve. These parties are wild. Drugs were available, but the contract specified no drugs. I can't book jobs for the models if they're high, bad for business, bad for reputation. Asia's job was to walk around being the pretty girl she is. She was a zombie, certainly not able to be the jubilant hostess.

She looks at me bewildered.

Just as I was about to escort her ass out, Javon enters with two drinks in tow.

He looks from Asia to me. "Is everything ok?"

"No, she was popping pills like popcorn. I reminded her about the 'no drug' policy."

"That was an aspirin I gave her earlier. I was bringing her a drink."

I don't believe him. My face I'm sure contorted to show this.

He hands her one of the drinks, giving me the other. "Since I am a gentleman, you can have mine. I'll get another."

"Your ass is never a gentleman. You have no concept of what that is or entails."

Javon looks at Asia, "You look good, Asia."

She doesn't respond.

I take a sip from my drink. It was good, kind of fruity and sweet. "You softening up, Javon? I was expecting something stronger from you. Some gin, a cognac."

"Ain't nothin' soft about me. Not even my dick." He winks at me.

"Asshole."

"Asia, you straight?" Javon asks.

She nods.

"Landon and I are going to have some fun down the hall. Rocco is downstairs if you need anything." Javon grabs my hand, escorting me out the door.

"We're not having anything. We do need to go down the hall to talk," I whisper being cautious of my surroundings, which was flooded with onlookers.

"Lead the way."

I head to the den located in a less populated area of the house. It was customary for us to have a room, normally a den, to conduct business at the parties. The room is set up like an office with a table, safe, couch, and a desk with a lock. In the room, we secured money as well as held all the collected cell phones, coats, and confidentiality agreements.

I took another sip from my drink, "What's going on?"

"What do you mean?"

"Asia is off. She got more going on than a headache.
"

He scrunches his shoulders. "Nerves, I guess."

"Javon what is Asia here to do?"

"To show guests a good time."

"How?"

There's a knock on the door before Rocco enters. He has a flunky with him scantily dressed in a black skirt that doesn't cover her yellow ass. Her white bustier is sheer, showing her erect nipples. Her hair pinned in a messy bun, lips pink. She's carrying a tray with drinks and cigars.

"That'll be all Natalia."

She places the tray on the table and then turns to leave. Rocco grabs her butt check.

She giggles before switching away.

Rocco turns to me, giving me the same glower as before in my office. "Landon."

I finish the drink I had, grabbing a similar drink off the tray. "Rocco."

Javon takes a seat in the swivel chair. "As you were saying, Landon."

"What are Asia's requirements?"

"To service guests."

"That's not what she was interviewed for."

"She chose to make some extra cash in between modeling gigs." Javon lights the cigar. I hated smoke.

"So she decided to be a prostitute. What about the other girls?"

He puffs his cigar. "Most of them did."

"The ones that didn't?"

I make the mistake of looking over at Rocco who is still giving me a death look.

"They are looking for other agencies." Javon puffs.

I take a drink. "So you gave them an ultimatum, forced them to be call girls."

"Does anyone look forced or being held against their will? The door is open. They're here because they want to be here."

I take another drink, starting to feel the effects of the alcohol. Javon was right. I was pissed he used me under false pretenses to get girls, but they choose to be here. The door was open. The ones who didn't want to sleep their way up to the top, had morals left.

Javon kisses me, I kiss him back. Rocco comes behind me, hands roaming all over my body. Oddly I was turned on, excited about the prospects. My clothes disrobed without any objections.

Javon sits in the chair, I bend over taking his dick in my mouth. Rocco comes behind entering me slow. Turns were had on me. They passed me around twisting and turning my body in every position. Double penetrations Rocco laying back in the lounge me on top him. He on top of me, both in and out, I am a see-saw. Treating me as a Vanessa Del Rio apprentice, they show me no mercy. So many things happening, who was I becoming? Dangerous game I was playing.

I knew I had to get away from them, somehow break all business ties.

24

Giving Something Up

"Melania, my favorite hoe."

"Landon, not today."

Paying no attention to her request, "What's the matter, you still lonely?

"Are you still jealous? By the way, Eric's tongue knows how to melt away a girl's troubles."

"But he isn't a Braxton is he?"

Her body stiffens.

I laugh. "You really fell for that joker?"

She sighs.

"You thought you were Julia Roberts and he was Richard Gere. Thought he was going to save your ass from the block. No boo, no fairytale there."

"Just shut up."

"His arrogant controlling ass is so overrated. Irks the hell out of me. I don't see what the hype is all about." I sip on my Cosmo.

"Bitch, please. Don't judge because I know your ass hopped on the same dick. Your son looks just like him."

I choked on my drink.

She laughs. "You rode the pony, trick. Your ass just didn't get off in time."

I take another drink.

"You're the real sheisty bitch. Fucking your girl's man? Even I haven't done that."

"It wasn't like that," I say defensively.

"It never is."

"It was an accident."

"So was me fucking Paul."

"That was different. You purposely went after him. That's why your ass got burned."

"Paul was a free agent. He was only committed to himself. It was fair game. You and I were after the same thing, his money. Honestly, I really went after him because of the way you approached me, like you were Queen B and everyone was supposed to bow down to ya ass. I didn't even have to try with him."

I groan. "For the record, I never wanted Braxton. I just didn't want him to hurt my friend, especially since your were fucking him. What happened was an alcohol disaster."

"Braxton, he has some good qualities. Dick is damn good. Definitely, has that evil side. I liked him because I knew he wasn't all caught up with this shit. He talked to me, listened, even took me out to nice places. He was safe, but he had the means to offer the best of both worlds."

I roll my eyes.

"Also for the record, I haven't fucked him in a while. He's been a good little doggy. Your girl got him locked down. And he let me know it wasn't happening."

I laugh. "I still don't like you."

She laughs also. "I don't like you either, hooker."

"No, I'll take the title of Queen Bitch, hooker never. That title belongs to you."

"Hmm, you and I are both hooked up with the same slimy ass motherfuckers. We both have sex with each of them and we get paid. We own the same title. You are just what you think you're not." She gets up and heads to the dance floor.

"I am not a hooker."

25

Do Your Worst

Braxton rushed through my front door as I opened it. "Where's Eric?"

"Upstairs."

He starts his rant, "What kind of shit are you trying to pull?"

I had called Braxton up requesting he take little Eric for a while. I didn't want to leave my baby, but I had to get my life in order. I had to regroup get my head in order. So many things were going on. I was beginning to feel like I was sinking. I needed to strategize. I had to break away from Javon and Rocco, protect my assets, myself. I booked a flight to Aruba in hopes to rejuvenate.

"Calling impromptu, saying you need me to get Eric."

"Well, he is your son."

"I know he is and I am taking responsibility for my son. It's the way you do things, Landon. You calling at the last minute demanding that I take him without notice. That's what I won't be dealing with."

"Whatever."

"It ain't no damn, whatever. You upset my wife. You know I'm trying to work things out with Yasmin."

I roll my eyes.

"Well with a child comes responsibility."

"Landon, what's your point?"

"Just like you have things to do, so do I."

"I didn't say I had things to do. I never have a problem getting him."

"Well, we can agree your tirade is unnecessary then."

Braxton looks at me. "What the hell is going on with you? You look a mess."

"You're not so great looking either."

He softens his tone. "Seriously, talk to me. What's going on?"

"I'm going to get Eric's things."

He grabs my arm. "Landon you don't look like yourself. You have dark circles under your eyes like a raccoon."

"What I do is none of your concern."

"Yes it is when it is affecting my son. Obviously, you can't take care of him."

"Don't tell me what I can't do. I am taking care of my son. You're the one having a fit because you had to come get him. Fuck you. Don't worry about Eric I will handle it myself."

"Landon, stop it!" He says through clenched teeth.

"Bastard! Get the hell out. Accuse me of being unfit. Asshole! I hate your ass."

He holds his hands up in surrender. "I apologize."

I unsuccessfully try to hold the tears in, "I love my son."

He gives me an awkward hug and I push him away. "You're right. I know you do."

"Fuck you. Leave. Goodbye. I won't call you anymore. You don't have to worry about Eric. Anything he needs I'll take care of."

He takes in a few deep breaths. "Landon, I apologize. I will take Eric. You can call me anytime. I don't have a problem taking him. I was only requesting you give me a heads up."

"Life doesn't work like that."

Braxton is standing glowering at me.

"I told you to leave Braxton."

"Get Eric and I will."

"I told you don't worry about it."

"I don't feel like this shit. In the future, like we agreed, just take Eric to my parents' house."

I wipe the tears from my eyes.

Braxton softens his approach. "Landon we need to get along. I'm sorry about earlier. We both have animosity towards each other, but Landon you can talk to me. I know something isn't right with you."

As much as I needed someone to confess to here was my opportunity, but Braxton though was not the one. He is so damn judgmental even though he has scandals of his own. Besides, he wouldn't even understand.

"I'm fine." I lied.

"Are you still dealing with Rocco and Javon?"

"What are you talking about?"

"The parties."

"You know about the parties?"

"Landon." He says letting me know he was tired of the games.

"Braxton you dealt with Javon. You knew he was in some shit."

"Not on a business level. I knew he supplemented his income, but I thought all of his business was legitimate with a few exceptions. I didn't know all the other shit he was into. I was around, but not all the damn time."

"What do you mean other shit?"

"Groupies always hang around athletes. Let's just say I knew about the escorting of women. I still don't or care to know the depth of his business."

"You didn't pay for Melania?"

"No, I didn't. I don't pay for sex."

"She must have liked your ass, her cost was steep too. You must feel special you got the number one call girl oversampled goodies for free."

He grips his hands into fists, "Landon, you really know how to piss me the fuck off."

I chuckle.

"You need to stay away from Javon and Rocco."

"Aww, listen to you sounding concerned." I mock.

"Landon, I'm serious. Javon is into a lot of things you don't need to be involved with."

"Really and what is that? You just said you didn't know the depths of his business."

"I did not come over here to play games with your ass today. You know everything. Forget it. I'm 99% sure you're involved somehow anyway."

"How did you find out about Javon's affiliations?"

"Word gets around."

"So that's why you stop dealing with him?"

"Yeah that and that motherfucker tried to fuck my wife."

"Anyone could see that. Yassy has a lot of admirers. I still get people asking me for a hook-up." I knew I was wrong, but he called me unfit and I do hold grudges.

"You really make someone wanna choke you."

"The same goes for you," I annunciate each word.

"You are Eric's mother. I don't want to see anything happen to you. I do take responsibility for Eric. I just ask in the future that you give me some notice. You know I got Eric. Right now things with Yasmin are fragile. You caught me off guard right as we were making progress. Your phone call just complicated things."

"Yas, being nice? She let you in the bed?"

"Landon, that's none of your damn business."

"Oh, dang my bad. Yas got horny. I knew it was only a matter of time. Now I know why she was so damn cranky."

He ignores me, "Landon just give me a little heads up. I have to get things back on track with her."

"Aww, you're trying to prove your love and commitment."

"Landon, what happens between Yasmin and I are our business. What I do to rectify this relationship or what transpired is not your business. I'm tired of your condescending remarks. I don't have shit to prove to you. All you need to know is I love my wife. That hook-up shit you did with her and Chauncey in the past, I didn't forget that shit. You can try to be manipulative if you want, it won't end nicely. For the last time, don't fuck with my marriage."

"Braxton calm down. I'm glad she is allowing you in. Take my advice, be patient. She's stubborn, but you can work it out. Watch your jealousy and outbursts."

"How long will you be gone?"

"I don't know."

I went upstairs to gather little Eric and his things. When I came back Braxton was by the door ready to go.

"Hey, little man." He reaches for Eric.

Eric goes without a problem.

I hated seeing the image of my baby with Braxton. The image was wrong on so many levels. It wasn't natural. Eric Ayres the 6'8" center for the Washington Wizards earned that title. Their interaction was much more genuine. Damn DNA. Braxton loved Eric, but his responsibility came from force. Eric deserved the title. I wish Eric would be a part of his life. Their bond was real and I know my baby was missing out on a lot. From Eric he would have learned how to be gentle, charismatic, genuine, honest, responsible, so many qualities I took for granted.

What really hurt was little Eric constantly asking about his daddy. Since he witnessed our fight, my baby has become scared of him. I had to tell my baby he wasn't coming back. "Daddy be bad," he would say. Other times, I could see he was confused, actually missing Eric. I hated to see that. Eric's image tarnished, both he and my son suffering an enormousness loss.

"Mommy baby, can I have kiss?" I walk over to kiss him.

"Love Mommy." Eric hugs me.

"Mommy loves you."

"Alright, I have Eric. He'll be fine. Settle any business you have with Rocco and Javon, Landon."

I nod.

26

I wish I could say the two weeks in Aruba did me some good, cleared my mind. The only thing it did was remind me of my mistakes. I did a lot of reflecting, but never came up with a solution for dissolving my business ties.

The first thing I did wrong was choose Aruba. I should have selected a venue I didn't have emotional ties to. The first week all I thought about was how this was Eric and my special place. It was the first time we were intimate in that way, the first time I ever told a man 'I love you.' It's where I was married. Aruba is where I discovered, in truth, I did love Eric. Too little, too late because rightfully so, he hated my ass now.

The second week I thought about my sister. I really messed that up. There was no excuse for fucking him. Braxton, from day one, had her heart. Yes, she had other relationships, but not like the one with him. My girl was giddy, secure and coming out of her shell. I see now that I was jealous that he had influence over her. It didn't matter that it was a positive change. When I saw him out with Melania it was the ammunition I needed to end the relationship. Having sex with him was never my intent. I do know Braxton loves my sister.

I decided I was just going to tell Javon I wanted

out of the business. I was just going to give them 90 days to find another partner. I sat across from Javon at Jacques Bistro. Anxious to get it over, I begin to speak.

"Javon, we need to discuss our business."

"Are you Landon Taylor?" a tall lanky nerdy male who reminded me of the Indian character in The Big Bang Theory approached.

"Yes."

"You've been served." A processor hands me forms to sign and then hands me a huge envelope.

He walks off like he gave me a compliment, not a care in the world.

Javon laughs. "Who suing you? What you do?"

"You are an ass. I don't know. I don't have x-ray vision."

I pull out the contents and review the papers. I couldn't do anything. I dropped the papers and

grabbed my head.

Javon nosy ass picks them up to review. "Damn, Eric isn't playing with your ass. This some when a man's scorned shit. We gotta get your money up."

Eric filed a lawsuit for lost wages, emotional distress, false pretenses, any and everything he could. He wanted me to pay him 20 million dollars. I wanted to contact him, tell him I would pay some restitution, but not 20 million dollars. From the rumors circulating, I wasn't surprised about getting sued just the amount. From my last encounter, I knew Eric was a loose cannon. The vacant look in his eyes had me more than spooked. Eric was a crazed maniac. I heard how he was in a downward spiral. Everyone is looking at me like I'm the cause. Okay, I helped, but Eric has other psychological issues. Poor Eric, he had so much going on. The nursing facility where his grandmother resided called expressing their condolences. Little Eric asks more for him, calling him his other daddy. What a web of deceit.

"I don't need this shit."

"Well you got this shit. We got to step it up. Speaking of which, I'm glad you brought up the business. Rocco is still upset about you stealing clients."

"Javon, I really don't feel like hearing about Rocco. I didn't steal anything. I was trying to make money."

"Using our connections without getting permission? That's classified info. You broke the client confidentiality agreement which is a privacy violation and you have to be fined. "

I pick up the papers, "Javon, as you see I have enough going on without you and Rocco's shit."

"Don't worry, Landon. I'm going to make it simple. You breeched our client's agreement. Punishment is 60 percent of your profits, retroactive for two months."

"Hell fucking no! How the hell is he going to go from demanding 40 percent to 60 percent? You both lost your damn minds."

"Landon you don't have the option to negotiate. That's it."

"I'm not giving you shit."

"You don't have any options. Eric suing your ass, you need the money so you're in a bind."

"If you know I need the money, why you cutting my profits?"

"You forced my hand when you started cutting into my profits."

"Are you forgetting my real estate business is what keeps everything afloat?" I say victoriously.

He chuckles. "For now we will leave things as they are."

"I thought so."

*

I wanted out, but I couldn't leave. In addition to Eric's lawsuit, I had accrued a massive amount of debt. Shopping became my vice. I had a ball shopping, buying up stuff like I lost my mind. Had to fill the void, furnish my new space.

I hadn't consulted with my accountant on several huge purchases and was now facing an IRS debt. My actions were never intentional but the crap was catching up with me. I was losing control. Mommy would be so disappointed.

As I sat in a daze on the sofa sipping on my Long Island Iced Tea, the party as usual was congested with sex craved socialites. I tried to smile, hide my dismay. After a while, I gave up. Going home was never an option, there I would only sulk. Javon would occasionally bring me a drink. I greedily drank, finally beginning to unwind. Soon, I did go to the dance floor when my theme song came on. I love Rihanna…

> I want you to be my sex slave
> Anything that I desire
> Be one with my femin-ay
> Set my whole body on fire

"Suck my cockiness, Lick my persuasion," I sang. Someone comes behind me, I begin a slow

grind, up and down his body. My short skirt and frilly top gives him access to my body. His long fingers find their way to my clit, hand cups my breast. The alcohol my aphrodisiac, his touch electrifying, I spread my legs to allow him access to my jewel. The stranger wastes no time plunging his fingers in and out of me. I twirl my hips squeeze my jewel tight trying my best to hit that spot. His dick gets hard, in a matter of seconds I am ushered to a corner. The thrill, I pay no attention to my surroundings. I ached for relief. I turn around to see the stranger with the magic fingers only to reveal that it's Chris. Normally, I would be repulsed by him, but the way he cupped my pussy and his fingers were hitting my spots, I stayed.

Incoherent, I find myself in the voyeur room. I know there are many eyes on me. Fittingly, I give them a Landon presentation. My body felt possessed, my mind a cloud. I remember using sex toys of all kinds, anal balls, dildo, nipple clips, rabbits, and a butterfly. I perform all types of sexual acts on myself. My orgasms so strong, I am breathless. My orgasms added to my nymphomaniac actions.

I staggered out of the room searching for a place to lie down, for me to get my head together. I had to go. Too much happening, no more drinks, go home. I felt myself getting sick, I had to lie down. I remember the hallway seemed so long with a lot of doors. The first door I opened, there was a girl being beaten with a whip. I remember seeing blood. She smiles at her master. The master grabs the girls head, forcing it on his cock. She gags, but never tries to stop him. I back out the room to continue my search for a bed.

The next room I enter, I am instantly paralyzed. There's a girl, a young girl, no more than 16 years old being held down. One guy holds her arms down, the other spreads her legs, while the third is fucking her roughly. Her screams being muffled by the guy that's fucking her, showing no mercy. Tears are streaming down her face, her eyes pleading. I try to stop them, say something, nothing will come from my mouth.

Javon walks up on me, his presence frightening me. He guides me out of the room and closes the door behind. We end up in another room. He hands me another drink. My eyelids feel so heavy.

I felt so light-headed. Tears rolled down, I don't know why I was crying.

When I look up, I see a girl in the room. Don't know who she is or where she came from. She looks worn and tired, hair tamed though, pulled in a neat ponytail that hung low. The girl holds a spoon of white substance up to me, "Just take a hit. It will help you get through."

I was in a low place, but I knew the last thing I needed was to get hooked. I shook my head no.

"You sure, you're not going to get addicted after one sniff. You just look like you need to take an edge off."

"I'm sure."

"Fine," she takes the spoon and takes a hit. I saw the emotion on her face go from shock from the potency of the dusk to a relaxed ecstasy. Her eyes closed and I saw her body begin to sway with the music. Just like that, her troubles look so far away, tempting, I took another sip of my vodka. It burned as it slid down my throat, but unlike her, I didn't get a euphoric feeling. My troubles were still there. I wanted to be numb, I wanted to rewind the clock, but I knew I would eventually wake up from this alcohol, from the drugs if I indulged, and my problems would still be there. I decided to indulge in the lesser of the two evils, alcohol would be my drug for now. Javon came over offering me another drink.

I take it. He is talking, but I don't hear him. I felt him. I wanted to push him away, but I really didn't have the energy.

My clothes were taking off.

Asia enters the room. Javon hands me a drink. When I'm done drinking he begins kissing me. Asia sucks my breast. My hands are roaming, my intent was to feel all over Javon, but they are on Asia. I am fascinated by the softness of skin, the swell of her breasts. Soon positions change. Asia kisses me while Javon fucks me. I never stop them. Not even when Asia small mouth licks my clit. My mind was in a fog. What the hell did he give me?

Flashes of kisses with Asia, her finger in me, pumping slowly come to me. Followed by more flashes of my head between Asia's thighs licking her as sensual as she did me. Images of Javon laying on the bed stroking his dick. Even a vaguer memory of a shower.

Exhausted, I'm too tired to move, let alone fuck. My head hangs on the pillow. I vaguely see Javon walk up on me, but I feel him sticking a metal object up my nose. I jerk back try to fight him. He's too strong. My heart beating to fast what the hell was he doing to me?

"Relax" he soothes.

I tried to blow my nose but it was useless, my body reaction was to inhale. When I did, I felt a strong burning sensation followed by euphoria. Energy surged through my body. I remember him sticking his dick in my mouth telling me to suck it.

Someone was in between my legs. The room was spinning. I'm barely able to lift my head. I lay back. My mind told me to move, leave, but my legs didn't cooperate. I felt the stranger pat my pussy down with a substance. I felt a tingle before it went numb. The stranger plunged in me so hard my head hit the wall. Even crazier, I didn't feel the pain. I don't feel him plunging in me now. As I lay flat on my back being fucked by a stranger, Javon stands over top of me and shoves his hard dick in my mouth before it all went black.

I woke up, my vagina aching, body aching, cold chills, the room a fog. It was too bright. I attempt to open my eyes, but I can't. I feel the burning feeling in my nose before I blackout again.

Dreams were meant to be sweet, mine were haunted with battered girls no older than 16, being broken, bruised, drugged and raped. Multitudes of men outnumbering the girls 10 to 1, all wait for their turn. Mouths covered, pain being felt, their eyes vacant, yet begging to be rescued.

One girl, not fully developed with shoulder length brown hair, dimples, carefree, pretty smile, round pretty innocent face now dark, same lost vacant eyes, strung out and calling death to rescue her. She looks directly at me. Her mouth isn't covered. She's begging me to "please" help her.

27

Love Yourself

"Landon, what has happened to you?" She cries.

My head is pounding. Her voice is too loud. I'm home. I don't remember how or when I got here. My body aches.

She rants, "I raised you better than this!. This is not acceptable. You need to go away. What did you do? How did this happen? I can't believe you let yourself go like this. Who are you? What are you on? Landon Alise Taylor?!"

I remain still laying on my stomach in the bed.

"Have you seen yourself, Landon? When was the last time you bathed?"

I don't know.

"Answer me, Landon."

My lips and throat dry, sore. I can't.

"Landon, how the hell did this shit happen? We don't do weak. You know this. Is this over Eric? You did not let a man bring you down like this. God no!"

Still I lie there, unresponsive, wishing she would leave me alone. Just let me lay.

"Landon, do you hear me talking to you? You will get yourself together."

'Ok," I solemnly respond.

"Your father can't see you like this. Landon, you are to remain in control at all times," she rationalizes. "You have to get up and take a bath. Do something with your hair. It's matted and what the hell is that in it?"

I close my eyes. My head is ready to explode.

Finally, she softens her voice, "Honey, what happened? Talk to me, please."

I look at her. I don't even know how or where to begin. Silence is best.

"I should have been here. I didn't realize you were struggling. Landon, I love you so much. You're all I have. Baby, what's wrong? We're going to get through this. You and I...like we always do. Baby, please talk to mommy." She cries.

I was too tired to respond. I wanted to confess everything to my mother. Tell her to get me out, but the shit I was into was far too much for her.

She leaves me for a few minutes.

She talks slowly, "Landon, you and I will be taking a trip tomorrow. You're going to take a sabbatical. In the meantime, your father and I will care for Eric."

I blink hoping she realized that was my way of saying yes.

That night mommy stayed with me. She bathed and attempted to feed me. It was useless. I didn't have an appetite and everything came out both ways. The chills in combination with the night sweats were the worst. It was a sleepless night for both of us. The next morning, we took a flight. On the plane, mommy read the local paper. Mommy panicked when she thought I was having a nervous breakdown because my body began to shake. I began to cry.

In the paper, was a photo of a 16-year-old missing girl named Janay Watkins. Shoulder length, brown hair, dimples, carefree, pretty smile, round pretty innocent face, but eyes that were vibrant. I couldn't read the article. I prayed for Janay, prayed she was safe. Prayed Javon wasn't holding her hostage.

Mommy had reserved a room for me at New Beginnings treatment facility in Mountain Springs, Colorado. There, I found out I had traces of cocaine, ecstasy, mollies and a variety of other drugs I had never heard of before. The withdrawal process was the worst: hallucinations, nausea, diarrhea, palpitations, just to name a few. The aggravating part was sitting through counseling admitting I had an addiction to drugs I didn't willingly take. I wanted to scream, "I was drugged!" But I definitely couldn't confess that. No one would believe that. It would be dismissed as classic addict denial. Besides, that would open up another can of worms. So, I sat in group sessions and confessed to addictions I didn't have. Judging from the symptoms and side effects, I realize Javon's ass has been drugging me for a while. Now I realize he was manipulating me and I fell right into his trap.

I was institutionalized for a few weeks. One of the requirements was for me to see a psychiatrist. My mother still assumed I broke down over my relationships with Yasmin and Eric. Yeah, they were factors, but not *the* factor. I dare not tell her the real reason behind my anxiety. My psychiatrist prescribed Ativan and Zoloft. Detox only made me want to run to a dealer to go back into my haze. Confronting Javon, who was hunting my ass, was enough to send me spiraling. Of course, since I vanished without a trace, he was furious. I lied saying I had a family emergency. Javon, who was always cocky, now had a god-like complex. He wanted his money. I knew he was pissed. Due to my absence, he couldn't continue to feed me those drug induced cocktails to get his way. He couldn't get into my head and make me a slave like the others. Without a question, he and Rocco were dangerous. I had to play smart. Take control of the situation. I knew I couldn't just blow-up and act a fool. As difficult as it was, I pretended all was well.

Over a month later, Janay was still missing. I was at a loss. What was I supposed to do? I couldn't contact the police and say she was at a sex party of horny celebs having sex and being drugged. That was weeks ago, who knew where she was. But, not doing anything wasn't right either. Prior to going to the detox center, I never had a desire for drugs, but the pressure was building. I needed something to take the edge off. Sleep meant nightmares. I quickly became a pill popping mess. My dreams were still haunted by Janay. I did break down and ask Javon about her. Javon told me he hadn't seen her since the party. In my gut, I knew he was lying.

Using the love of money and fame to magnetize, before you could blink, you were under his control. Slyly drugging them, like me, setting them up to become obedient, subservient sex slaves. The door was open, but he had there mind. Master pimp, master manipulator, he didn't need wire hangers or to slap them around. But, they experienced the worst abuse that years of psychological treatment would not fix. They, we, are his prisoners.

I wish I took heed to Melania's warning. I will contact her. See how she walked away from this mess.

28

My Prison

I checked my mail which had been mounting for the last few weeks. The first piece of correspondence I opened had me sick. I was being audited by the IRS, citing "undocumented funds." Basically, they suspected me of money laundering.

My phone buzzes. I look to see if it was Javon. Since my hiatus, he's been blowing up my phone. He didn't want me, he wanted his damn money, which I was holding. He owed me that and more. While I was away the parties continued. I had $1 million of *his* dollars.

Like a dumbass, everything was in my name so I'd take the fall. I thought I was in control when I'd been manipulated like a ventriloquist. I can't believe I got myself caught up in this shit. Then again, what the hell was I thinking? How am I going to get out of this shit? Damn. I should call Kevin, but what am I going to say? How can I explain to him I got caught up in laundering money, prostitution, drugs and a list of other crimes I'm not even aware of?

My phone buzzes with another message from Javon telling me to call him. I know I said I was going to play it cool, but the IRS threw that rationale out the window. Javon's ass wasn't getting any money. He owed me for all the grief and shit. My Gmail account had a new message from an unknown address. I was just about to delete it until I read the headline.

Breaking news: Body of Melania Vasquez found.

The body of the email contained a link to the local news station. I sat motionless as the video played.

Baltimore Police say a woman was found dead in a Highlandtown home overlooking Patterson Park on Friday morning.

> *The woman, 26, identified as Melania Vasquez was found at about 7:30 a.m., inside a home in the 200 block of S. Ellwood Ave. with "trauma to her upper body," police said. Police did not provide additional details but a neighbor, who did not want to be identified, said the property had been vacant for years.*
>
> *In the rear of the home, crime scene tape blocked off a fenced-in patio. A chair from an outdoor furniture set was against the home below the kitchen window, which was open. From the front of the home, nothing appeared out of the ordinary except for two marked police SUVs parked on the street.*
>
> *If you have any information on this case, please contact police at 410-399-1200*

This had to be a hoax. But when I checked Melania's public Facebook page, it was flooded with "Rest in Peace" posts. . We had our rivalry, but I never wanted her dead. Scanning her pictures, I saw pictures of her with family, so different than her party girl persona. Make-up free, but pretty nonetheless. She was carefree. Her eyes looked happy, even innocent. The picture that touched me the most was the one she had with her son. Her son looked no older than three. She was laying lazily on the grass, throwing her son in the air. Her son is smiling, reaching for her, love in both of their eyes.

Her innocent son will now grow up motherless. Tears rolled down my cheek thinking of how I knew he was wondering why his mama wasn't home. I'm sure he asked for her, wanted more kisses, hugs. So innocent not understanding she wasn't coming back. My body shook, fear for her, for my son.

What if he decided to research his mother? Thanks to the internet, the image of her that would be painted would be a whore that got strung out on drugs chasing the fast life, that she abandoned him. His father had already relinquished his parental rights (the reality of having kids by these athletes who don't give a shit), now both of his parents are gone before the age of four. My heart ached imagining what that would do to him. I prayed someone came to him, before he became another lost child in the system. I prayed he had someone to shape him or explain to him his mama loved him.

I know I heard the news, read the paper, but two days later, I still couldn't believe she was gone. I had to see for myself. I did an internet search to find the funeral home. I knew her friends, especially Ty, would call me every bitch there was for showing my face. I deserve it. I made it a point to degrade Melania every time I saw her. Trying to be incognito, I wore a long wrap wig to conceal my face and a baggy pantsuit. When I pulled up, I expected an abundance of cars, but there wasn't.

Walking in, I braced myself for ridicule, but it was needless, none of her friends were there. People were there casually talking about current events. It was as if she never existed, forgotten already. Everyone content, except a woman sitting in a wheelchair by the ivory casket, grasping Melania's hand, silently willing her to come back. With hesitancy, I walk up to her. She never takes her eyes from her body, but she knows I'm there.

Voice low, she asked, "Did you know my daughter?"

"Yes."

"She really was a good girl."

That's what all mothers say, I thought. She continues, "She just loved fancy things. She thought it made her beautiful, thought it meant power, envy."

I didn't know how to respond. I shook my head although she never looked at me, picking at my fingers.

"She always loved the attention from people. Everyone, from the day she was born, always said she was pretty. Told her she could have the world, she believed it. She met the wrong people."

She reflects some more.

"My girl she didn't kill herself. I don't believe it." She says with conviction. "She didn't do this to herself.

For the first time, I looked at Melania and I gasped. I didn't mean to be so loud or cause a scene. My commotion ceased the talking and caused an older man to come over to check on her mother and make sure I didn't faint. Looking at Melania, I literally became sick. She was a shell of herself. The trauma had aged her. I know a drug user's appearance drastically changes, but looking at her she was traumatized. Her face looked swollen, her neck was dark. I could tell they tried to lighten it with make-up, but it was a disaster. Her entire face was caked with make-up. She appeared to be 46, rather than the short 26 years she lived. Lying before me was not the girl whose beauty I had come to realize I envied.

"I'm sorry, I didn't mean to…"

"How do you know my girl?"

"We worked together."

She finally looks at me. With her free hand she grabs my hand.

"She left me a little boy to raise. Do you have any kids?"

"Yes, a son also."

She blinks tears. "Mellie loved her son. She wanted so much for him."

The huge lump that forms in my throat renders me speechless and I didn't bother holding back the tears. "I'm so sorry we had to meet this way and I'm deeply sorry for your loss. Is there anything I can do? Do you need anything?"

She stares at me with intensity and squeezes my hand tight. "You be careful. I wouldn't want your mother to be sitting here next. You in the same business, No?"

"Yes ma'am."

She lets go of my hand, focusing her attention back to Melania, she begins humming a lullaby.

I ease my way from Melania's grieving mother. When I reach my car, I am so drained. All that fame, friends who talked about her on Facebook, said she would be missed. Yet, when it was all said and done, none of them were there. Gone, forgotten, just one of many casualties in the business which sadly resulted in death.

I imagined Melania starting out like Asia. Innocent, trusting people like me, only to end up being labeled a hoe, being judged. Like Asia, Melania wanted the fame, the glitter, the gold. Melania, like many, drugged, lost, and now dead trying to chase that dollar, unfortunately, would not be the last.

I'm so glad Yasmin never fell into that lifestyle with me. So glad she was smart enough to know from the beginning that lifestyle was a gamble, came with a lot of consequences, rules, sacrifices and was not a game. Although she wasn't talking to me, I knew if I ever needed her, she would be there. I had a real friend who I betrayed in the worst way. Yasmin was the friend I needed now.

29

Find A Way

For appearance's sake, I've been trained well. I put on my happy face to see Yasmin. Pushing my tremendous troubles aside, I went to see my nieces. They were only a few weeks old and I was anxious to see them again. I knew Yasmin was still struggling with forgiving me. She was cordial, but more importantly, she was happy. They had quite a few visitors, which was a good thing. No awkward silence and I could just observe. I missed Yassy's presence.

The twins, Raegan and Khouri, were gorgeous. Braxton was tolerable. Looking at him, I know finally, he loved my girl and was 1000 percent committed. Every time she made a move, he was right there making sure she wasn't overdoing it. If they didn't have the twins, Braxton would either have her in an embrace, holding her hand, or kissing on her. That was overkill, but, I was truly happy for them. The four of them fit and I pray that they worked out. Yassy deserved this.

*

You ever wish life had a fast forward button or a preview so you could get an idea of how things were going to turn out? Wish I had an idea of where I was going so I could prepare for the ride. It's nothing like being alone. Alone, you sit dwelling in mistakes, wishing for a do-over. Alone, you get depressed, no friends to rescue you from self-pity; no friends there to talk to or cry on their shoulder. I miss my Yassy, my only true friend.

I tried to do something to try to get my mind off of my disastrous life. Visiting Kevin was the only thing I could think of. Maybe I could talk to him. I knock on the door to his home.

Kevin startles me and I drop my purse. All of the prescription drugs I had fell out. I scramble to pick them up.

"Landon, what's all this?"

"Nothing."

"Landon, talk to me. Why do you have all of those pills? What illegal activities are you into?"

"What?" I say, appalled.

"Kevin, these are vitamins."

"Landon, I can't help you if you don't tell me."

"Kevin, look at me. I've been stressed."

He looks at the bottles in my hand. "That's a lot of bottles you have. Multivitamins only require one bottle."

"I have an iron and vitamin D deficiency. I'm taking a multivitamin along with the iron and vitamin D to build my immune system."

"Yeah, you do look worn."

"You don't look so great either," I snap back.

"You know I'm telling the truth. Back to you, why didn't your doctor just give you one pill instead of giving you all of these?"

"I don't know, Kevin. I'm not a doctor and neither are you. You have a law degree. You're use to research, look it up."

"I'm just trying to look out for you."

"How?"

"Landon, are you into anything illegal?"

"Kevin, really, like what? You think I'm selling pills? Me?"

"I don't know what's going on with you. That's why I'm asking."

"Kevin, my sister isn't talking to me because I had a baby with her husband. My ex-husband is trying to sue me for emotional distress. My parents lecture me every fucking time I go there and now I finally come to you to talk and you accuse me of being a drug dealer."

"Landon, I'm sorry. I know a lot is going on."

I put my hand up, "Goodbye, Kevin."

"Landon, I apologize. "

It was too late I was already out of the door.

30

Warning

"Landon, you fuckin' with my money. You want me to come put my foot in your ass? My money, don't fuck with my money! Landon do you think I'm playing games with your silly ass?!" Javon barks. After avoiding him, he finally corners me in my office.

"If you turn that over you get nothing. You think I'm going to take all the charges. You think I don't have proof, recorded conversations, pictures."

He laughs. "Oh you a Boss Bitch. That Queen Bitch, running things, giving orders."

Ignoring him, I said, "You got 30 days to get your affairs in order. I've had enough. Find another partner. I'm closing the business. As far as the money, consider it your price to buy me out."

"You don't run shit. I got tapes with you snorting, proof of your money laundering, and pictures of you with the missing girl." Javon pulls out his phone. There I am, on the screen having sex with the missing girl and Asia. I don't remember any of this. He had to have Photo-shopped it.

But this was mission accomplished because he had me shook.

"The police would like to see this."

"You were in that video too, Javon."

"That's the beauty of editing along with the time stamp. You were the last person to be with her and let's not hope the body is found. Your DNA is all over her body, her tongue. This was taken after the shower. I was all washed away and I have an alibi."

"Oh my God, you set me up!"

"Set up? No, I took precautions," he says smoothly.

"Fuck you!"

"You got a condom, I can," he whips out his dick.

"You dirty no good motherfucker."

"You want to suck it?"

"Javon, what do you want?"

"My money to start."

Truth was, I didn't have his money. I did some research on Melania and found out where her mother and little boy lived. They had been through enough. Her son already had the odds stacked against him. Melania would want her mother and son to be taken care of. With this lifestyle, life insurance, social security or pensions were not provided. I anonymously donated a decent house for her under a fictitious non-profit and set up a trust fund along with a monthly stipend to aid her mother in caring for him. The best $2 million I ever spent.

"I will pay you back in installments."

"What happened to that boss bitch? Now you want to negotiate? No bitch, I want my money now!"

I try to reason with him. "You know Eric has this lawsuit against me. My money is tied up. I need some time."

He's calm. "Like the 30 days you were giving me to get things in order?"

"I need a little more time than that."

"How much time?"

Shit. I panicked. How the hell was I going to pay back two million dollars? My ass was going to have to put the work in with my license and sell some houses, do something. In 60 days? Hell no. Not in 90 or 120 days either. I took a substantial loss of income with my divorce. Not even mentioning the money loss with Javon. The money I stashed away totaled $7.2 million. Eric was suing me for $20 million. I tried to settle for $2 million. It came as no surprise that he didn't accept. Originally, my mother represented me. Mommy wanted to play hardball and not settle so quickly, but I wanted this to be over. She couldn't understand I was wrong. Eric deserved to be rid of me. Between being ashamed of what I'd become and being drugged, thanks to the asshole before me, I hired other counsel. It took a lot of negotiations, but Eric finally settled for 5.2 million dollars. After attorney fees, I had a little over a million dollars left. I used a large portion of that to purchase a townhome for little Eric and I. My mother though, was still furious about me firing her. Our relationship is still strained.

"I can pay installments."

"No bitch, it don't work that way. You were such a bad bitch earlier running off at the mouth, you fucked yourself."

"I'm sorry. I just want out."

"No sorry's. You have two weeks to give me my money. As far as the business, it stays open till I say otherwise. The consultant biz, I want a cut of that two. The new rule, you are my employee. You get ten percent. Now get to work, bitch."

He leaves out of my office whistling.

Since Javon barged into my office, my anxiety has become unbearable. The pills weren't helping. Things were closing in. I was being tortured daily, unnerved by my many dreams of Melania. Janay was still missing and

Nakia Robinson

I felt my time was ending. They killed Melania, they'll kill me. I was scared I would be another Baltimore statistic whose body was left in an abandoned Baltimore city row home. It was common for criminals to murder someone in the suburbs and then dump them in Baltimore City to add to their growing homicides. Having to watch your back and look over your shoulder was not a way to live.

31

We Can Be New

Two weeks ended a month ago. I didn't have anything close to the two million dollars, not even a quarter. I thought about asking my parents. Yes, they had money, but to liquidate 2 million dollars meant I had to do some confessing. Admitting to my parents that I willingly turned my legal, profitable business into an illegal prostitution ring? There would be no defense. In my state of mind, I'd crumble at their cross-examination. I'd threatened my father in the past to get my way, but with $2 million dollars on the table, I knew my limitation. Most of all, I was so tired of being manipulative.

I jumped when I heard a knock at the door. I cautiously peak out of the peephole. It was a pleasant surprise to see Yasmin at my door. For the first time, I had happy tears.

"Yas?"

"Hello Landon, can I come in?"

"Yeah."

I watch as her eyes roam over my townhouse taking in my eccentric colors and décor. "Nice place, where's Eric?"

"Thanks. He's with daddy."

"Let me get straight to the point. I don't want to keep rehashing the past and hearing I'm sorry. You were wrong. And although this is hard for me, I forgive you."

"Yas…"

She stops me, "I forgive you, however our relationship will never be the same. Trust is a hard thing to get, but an easy thing to lose. With that being said, I will try to build a relationship with you. Crazy but true, you are my sister. Our kids have the same father. I don't think we can be as close as we were, but we can try to make this craziness as normal as possible."

"Thank you, Yassy," I cried.

We hugged.

I grab her hand. "Yassy, I'm really grateful that you're back in my life." I cry.

"What's wrong? I thought we were cool."

"I'm sorry. I just…I just feel real bad. I'm looking at your hand and see your ring is still off. I talked to Kevin and he told me it was over. I didn't want to believe it. I fucked up everything for you and the girls."

"Landon, first thing, my relationship with Braxton, whether there is one or not, is off limits. Braxton had a part in this mess. I've thought long and hard about my decision and I've made it. Again it's not any of your business."

"You're right, I apologize. I know your life has been difficult. I am truly, deeply sorry in the part I had in making it more difficult. I thank you for allowing me to have any part, big or small. I finally realize I wasted a lot of time being dumb, stupid and selfish. I hurt a lot of people in the process, especially you and Eric. For that, I will bear the pain for the rest of my life. You just don't know how ashamed I am."

"I believe you," Tears fill her eyes as well.

We hug before she leaves.

32

End of Time

I had something to be happy about. Things were looking up. There wasn't a second thought when I gingerly opened my front door a few hours later, smile still plastered on my face. My expression drastically changing once I saw the possessed look in his eyes.

He stares at me with so much hate. I know I deserve it but it hurts.

"You just think you can say sorry and all is forgiven?"

"I am sorry. I honestly never meant to hurt you."

"Shut the hell up!"

"I thought ... I - I - I wanted him to be yours," I stuttered.

"Landon, you ain't nothing but a gold-diggin' hoe. Tony told me to stay away from yo' ass! He said how you was nothin' but a high class escortTrifling Bitch!" Then he slapped me across my face with so much force I thought my neck snapped. I swear he's trying to slap the skin off my face. I hold my stinging face while checking for blood.

"My career is over because of you! I'm a fucking joke! You fucked the damn league and even fucked my teammates in my house," he slaps me again just as hard as before.

"Eric, I swear I didn't fuck any of your teammates in your house," I pleaded.

He returned a sinister laugh.

"I didn't."

He grabbed me and pushed me hard into the wall saying, "Bitch, you gonna look me in the face and still lie to me? Lie and tell me you ain't fuck anyone in my house and then smile in my face. You gonna stand here and tell me you ain't fuck nobody else while I was married to your trifling ass?"

I put my head down.

He yanks it up, hard, "Answer me bitch!"

His eyes are dark, nothing but pure hate for me; so much callous hate I caused. I close my eyes.

He grabs my face, "Open your goddam eyes and look at me!"

I admit I have done him dirty on so many levels. His anger and hurt is justified. I honestly didn't set out to hurt him. It was never my plan. I got caught up and I made one bad decision after another. Before I knew what happened or realized the magnitude of my actions, it was too late. I just did what I knew and rode the wave. Unfortunately, that wave was too big, too powerful, and I couldn't ride the tide.

"Landon! You hear me talking to you?" he slaps me again.

"You got a good laugh off of me, spent my money, and talked me like I was your puppet," another slap.

"Eric, I'm so sorry. I thought he was yours. I wanted him to be your son," I cried.

"You ain't nothing but a lying whore," he grabs me,

---

yanking my neck. "Landon, I'm going to ask you this and your ass better not lie. Do you understand me?"

"Yes," I croak.

"Why did you kill my baby?"

I swallowed hard. I was too scared to answer him; too scared to tell him the truth. I didn't want to tell him that I didn't know if the baby was his. I closed my eyes, debating whether or not I should tell him the truth, praying silence would be enough. Of course it wouldn't be.

He grabbed my jaws and said in a low chilling voice, "Open yo' mutherfucking eyes, look at me and answer my damn question."

I was so tired of the lies, so tired of the schemes and the running. I was tired of all this shit. I obey. I look him in the eyes as the tears roll down my face and respond, "I didn't know if you were the father."

He releases me. My words have his mind spinning as they set off a new war within him. He wanted me dead. He wanted me to pay. I shiver, scared to move, scared it would trigger him to act on his anger. Looking at him, I knew his mind was unraveling right before my eyes. His mind was gone. My truths struck something deep within. I wanted to move, run, do something to get away, but I couldn't, my movement would snap him from the delusion and disbelief he was in and focus his attention back to me. I stood still, careful not to make a move or a sound.

He began to rock back and forth slowly and in a low shrill voice said, "You took my career, my money. Now you tellin' me you took TWO kids from me?"

The next thing I knew he came at me full force, grabbing me by the neck and throwing me against the wall. My head hit the wall hard and I fell to the floor like a rag doll. I lay against the cold marble with my tears soaking the floor.

Eric paces the floor, talking to himself. "I don't believe this shit. This bitch. I should've listened to Nana,

now she gone. I don't have no kids. This bitch…kill her.
I got to kill her. She got the whole league laughing at
me. She gotta die. She took my kids. She took my kids."

My body tenses at the sound of his words.

Within seconds, he yanked me up in the air screaming, "Tell me why I should let you live!"

Sadly, I don't have any answers…no response.

"Just what I fucking thought! There *is* no reason.
Your ass needs to die."

Tears run down my face, my chest heaves in and out,
my legs ready to buckle.

Eric grabs my neck, I want to throw up, but nothing could come. His hands are sucking the air from me.
They are muscular and strong from years of dribbling the
basketball. My feet are barely touching my pretty marble
floor. He squeezes tighter. My eyes bulge from the pressure. My face hot is hot, swelling from a lack of oxygen.
He's killing me, slowly, painfully.

I squirm, struggling from being deprived from
oxygen, knocking any and everything down. The thump
from the photo frame snaps Eric from his trance. He
looks at the photo, then he looks at me and immediately
releases his grip as if the realization of what he is doing
hits him.

I fall to the floor gasping for air, holding my burning
chest. The tears burn my cheek and my head pounds.
I need to move, lock myself in a closet, do something
before he literally squeezes the life out of me. I try to
focus, I try to move, but I'm paralyzed from pain, lack of
oxygen. I look over to see Eric sitting on the floor, knees
up holding a picture. He's crying. His eyes scream hurt,
disbelief, so much pain. My pounding heart breaks, my
body in so much pain, I'm barely able to breathe. But
looking at him, I wish I could take all his pain…erase
me from his memory. I feel so horrible in so many more
ways as I look at him holding that picture.

I remember the day the picture was taken. It was little Eric's first birthday. My little baby loved me. He was my baby, but from the beginning Eric was more hands on with diapers and feedings. He was so proud. There were many days that I had spa days while they had father and son bonding days. I love my son, but Eric lived for him. He had just begun to walk. Lil' Eric grabbed a hunk of cake and took a bite. He lifted his little chubby arms to be picked up. I was not getting messy in my peach Prada romper, so Eric eagerly obliged, swooping him up in his arms. Lil' Eric tried to wrap an arm around Eric's neck while saying, "Ea... Dada, Ea... The photographer captured the moment of son feeding his father, his idol, cake. I always loved the innocence in my baby's eyes. The picture shows the adoration, the love he has for him. I recall the sweet memory and I hurt even more. I recall how after the photo was taken the photographer caught another of Eric kissing the son he thought was his and little Eric doing the same. It was a wonderful day; we were a family. The party, the cake fight afterwards, I wasn't even mad when they both smeared my pretty romper. It was all fun...but it was a lie.

Eric slowly gets up. I brace myself for more deserved pain. He stands over me, staring. He looks down at the photo, steps over me and then peacefully leaves out of the door with the photo in hand.

Oh my god, I feel so bad. Eric is so right, sorry would not change things. It would not erase the years he lost for being caught up in my lies. So much damage I've done. There was nothing I could do to make it right, being with me destroyed the man he was, turned him into a psychotic mess.

My life is a mess. Everything is closing in on me. The bitch called Karma has come back to take me out. Karma has many allies and too much ammunition. I don't have any fight left in me. So much has transpired in these last few weeks. I knew she would come back to make me suffer, break me down and leave me calling for death to rescue me.

My front door opens, I try to move, but my body is exhausted. Not sure how long I'd been down, I remained still, allowing the wetness of my tears to cascade across my marble floor. I don't look up until he steps in front of me. Dirty black steel toe boots are there.

"You thought I was playing with your ass!"

His voice is so powerful and menacing that my body trembles.

I don't move fast enough, the dirty black steel boots lift and come crashing down on my ribs. Then another kick to my stomach so severe and forceful, I slide to the other side of the room.

"I'm sorry," I cough and cry in agony.

"Sorry don't mean shit to me."

He grabbed my arm, pulling my 105-pound frame up like it was a mere fifteen pounds.

I wince from the pain.

He grabs my bruised neck and laughs, "You always liked it rough."

He holds my neck tight, but not tight enough to choke me. He taunts me instead.

"You were always a high price hoe who thought you were in charge. You thought you were a boss bitch. No, bitch! You were always a hoe. An expensive overpriced hoe!"

I cry.

"Pussy wasn't all bad, not the best. You served your purpose. For old time's sake, huh?"

I groan.

He laughs and pulls out his dick.

"No," I plead.

"If you ass knows what right, you better suck me dry and right. Now assume position."

I get on my knees. He walks up to me, his dick hard and ready.

"Suck my dick hoe. You never had a problem before. I give you your props. That tongue of yours was a great stress reliever. Like I said suck it right. I may have mercy on you."

I do as he requests sucking him for my life. He wasn't lying I'd done this many times before. I knew what to do to get him to release and within two minutes I was swallowing his sour cum.

He pulls out and smiles, "Damn, that was some good shit, but not enough for me to forget. Stand up."

I do. "I'm sorry. I was wrong," I babble.

"You damn right, you were wrong. You were a conniving hoe. You think I'm playing your ass. You think I'm just gonna let you play me? Bitch, you got me fucked up. Yo' ass is gonna pay."

"Please," I cried.

"Please what? Please don't hit you?" He smacks me, releasing his grip from my neck. "Please don't kick you?" He took his steel toe boot and kicked me in the back as I attempted to run. My knees buckled and I crashed down. I hear a pop in my right knee and pain immediately follows.

"Please don't do what?" His steel boot came down hard crashing into the side of my head. He stomped again, again, and again. I swear my ear rang, busted, and echoes began.

He was talking but I was in too much pain and his voice sounded so muffled. He grabs me, trying to stand me, but my knee was not allowing. I wobble. He pushes me up against the wall. My equilibrium off, I want to just fall to the floor, but I knew better.

"All the money you took from me. You think I'm

going to take it as a loss?"

"You're right. I'm sorry. Give me a couple of days to liquidate some funds," I plead.

"Oh now you want to make arrangements," he laughs. "There are no more options."

"Please, please, please. I'm sorry."

"Please don't what, bitch?" He kicks me in the stomach. If my body didn't absorb the blow, there would have been a hole in the wall.

I go down hard, coughing, mouth spewing blood.

He comes at me with no mercy at all. He continuously stomps on me. Each time, cracking bones

echo in my head, while the pain radiates throughout my body. Boom, Boom, Boom, Boom, Boom

Boom!

He finally stops, but I have no relief.

"Get the fuck up, Landon."

"I can't," I moan.

"Bitch, I said get the fuck up!" He grabbed my yellow shirt, now stained with red blood, ripping it in the process propping me up like a mannequin. My right knee was swollen, unable to bend. I force my weight to my left leg.

I cry out from pain.

"Look at me, bitch!"

I look up in time to see fire. At the same time, I feel my chest burn. I grab my chest trying to alleviate the sting, the burn, but it only intensifies. My hands are slippery, soaked with blood. I feel water running down my legs, I had peed on myself. Everything is in slow motion as my knees buckle, but the crash on the floor stuns me with new pain.

The steel boots are inches from my face. He bends down looks at me and spits right in my face. He chuckles before he takes his steel boot to kick me in the face. I slid across the room while he walks out of my door... But before saying

"Die, bitch."

It's true I've done a lot of things I'm not proud of, hurt people, said things, made a hell of a lot of mistakes. But show me a person who hasn't. Granted, a lot of what I've done was ruthless, even lacked morals, but not all was intentional. People are notorious for judging people. For example, people are quick to say gays are not of God and their lifestyle is wrong, yet these same people are living out of wedlock. They both are having sex out of marriage. I know I'm the main one. I admit me, Landon, my mouth, my actions are RECKLESS. Who are you to judge? Who am I to judge? Point being, you don't have any hierarchy over me and definitely don't have any room to judge. I'm not about to go get all religious quoting scripture, I only wanted you to see you can't always go by perception. What you see is not always as it is.

You had the facts, now you know my story. Yes, I should have been wiser. But, do you still think I deserve death?

"Things Are Not Always As They Appear......"

"As you know, we've done all we can for your daughter," a male voice says with sorrow.

"No, we do not know that. I want second, third, fourth opinions! I don't give a damn how many!" Mommy flusters. Give me a damn doctor who doesn't start a sentence with 'we've done all we can.'"

"Jackie, calm down," pleads daddy.

"I will not. How dare you remain calm when my baby is dying!"

"Mrs. Taylor," a female voice says with sincerity. "Landon experienced extensive trauma. She's been in this vegetative state for several days. We've run the full battery of tests, yet there still has not been any brain activity. The machines are keeping her alive at this point."

"Don't fucking say it! Don't you dare fucking say it! Do you know who the fuck I am? Do you know what I can and will do to this hospital if you attempt to remove her from life support? You will not. My daughter is alive. She responds to my voice. If you are not capable, then find a doctor who is."

"Mrs. Taylor, Mr. Taylor," the male doctor pleads.

"You will not. I will file every motion possible. I

will sue the hospital, every got'damn doctor who has touched my child. Get me the chief of staff now. I want my daughter moved to another hospital immediately."

"Jackie!"

"Get off of me, Lawrence!"

"Her heart is still beating, don't kill my baby. Please."

Moments later I hear another male voice.

"Mr. Taylor, Mrs. Taylor I am Dr. Parks, Chief of staff for Georgetown University Hospital. Your daughter is severely incapacitated."

He continues, "She will need extensive reconstructive surgery. The left side of Landon's face was shattered. She has a broken cheek bone, broken jar and eye socket. She will need orbital fracture surgery to realign her bones and restore normal eye movement. The surgery will also require titanium plates."

Mommy wails.

"Regrettably, this is the least of her problems."

"What are we dealing with? Please be as candid as possible," said daddy.

"Landon was shot in the chest with a .45 caliber gun. This gun carries a heavier velocity bullet. This bullet deforms on impact> It penetrated the chest wall and damaged her lung. . This has caused her to cough up blood, be very short of blood, and basically drown in her own blood."

"Oh my God."

The doctor continues. "An endotracheal tube was placed into her windpipe to help with breathing. The left lung has two lobes – upper and lower. The left lung has a nodule called the Lingula which is adjacent to the heart area. Landon was shot in the left lung."

There is a pause.

"As you know, while Landon was in surgery she was placed on a ventilator, but we were unable to remove the endotracheal tube due to her having several broken ribs. If the tube remains longer than several days complications can arise, the most common being pneumonia. Another complication a patient may develop is Deep Vein thrombosis or DVT, where the patient begins to develop blood clots. Landon has been in a vegetative state for eight days. She has developed both and her health is rapidly deteriorating."

"Diva, we have so much more to do. Don't leave me yet. We got some living to do, more adventures and chaos. Who would think we'd have kids? You got to play dress up with them. I love you, Land. Stay, please."

Yasmin brought out the best in both Braxton and I and we did the worst to her. I always admired her strength. I saw how her mom was towards her, but Yasmin never broke down. She did right even when Braxton broke her heart. I knew she was miserable, but she was there for me. I swear, when Little Eric came out and I saw him, my heart broke. I couldn't tell her, I couldn't tell Eric, so I had to keep up the façade. I guess I got my karma. Yasmin, my sister I've missed her so much this past year. She always had my back good or bad. This year has been miserable without my sister. I wish I could have slowed down maybe trusted sooner. Braxton he still irks the shit out of me, but I know he loves my sister. He's made plenty of mistakes was even more of hoe than I, but Yasmin got his ass in check. Go sis for accomplishing that task.

"I love you, lil' sis," said Kevin. . Kevin, my brother, he was annoying like any big brother, attorney to the core, yet I wouldn't have it any other way. I still don't trust his Yasmin clone, who he's now engaged too. Something isn't right with her. I just pray that she doesn't hurt him.

I wish I learned there is a difference between being smart and being manipulative.

While I had daddy throughout the years, I wouldn't say it was a benefit. I did love my daddy. He was an excellent provider, but he was also a cheater. I saw too much, was definitely exposed too too much and it affected me. I knew he loved me, but at the same time I didn't believe in his love. . I didn't believe he wouldn't hurt me. Catching him in numerous affairs, seeing mommy cry, hurt me and in turn caused me to resent him. It's ironic how what I resented, I became. I think he finally did stop cheating. . I hope so for mommy's sake. She's going to need him. .

My mommy, she is so strong and she raised me to be the same. I appreciate her instilling in me that I could be anything I wanted. I never doubted my self-worth. She was persistent in enforcing independence in me. . In her quest to make sure I'd never end up hurt or fooled by love, she exposed me to too much. I know she's tired from carrying all the hurt and pain she's endured over the years. I know she pretends work is enough, but it wasn't. She really wanted to be loved and know she was my father's one and only.

I hear the heart machine slowing more, the alarms going off. Mommy sobs far away, but clear. "Landon baby, don't leave Mommy, please. Baby, please don't leave me." I want to stay but it's so, so, so hard.

I can't take this pain. It's so easy for me to let go. The meds aren't helping, the more I let go, the freer I feel. My mind is filled and every cell in my body is in pain.

I don't want to die, but maybe I'm better off dead. If I live I will be a shell of myself. The idea of being disfigured… I've matured, but I'm still vain. Surviving as an ugly disfigured duckling…I can't. As if disfigurement isn't enough, my ass can possibly be facing laundering and prostitution charges. If I die, my baby won't be subjected to hearing how awful his mommy was or about all the scandals. My family would never reveal my truth. The idea of my baby visiting me in a jail, I couldn't bare it. I know mommy, daddy, and Kevin would do all they could to prevent jail time, but my ass was just in too deep. Javon crazy ass lurking around and Rocco had connections that ran deep. Not to mention the nightmares, images permanently embedded in my head for life. I would never rest.

I hear the doctors tell my family my organs are shutting down. I know they want me to stay, but the truth of the matter is I'm better off dead.

Little Eric, the only thing I did right. My baby, how I wished I could just hold him. Give him the manifold kisses he loves. He was always protective of me. The only boy I gave all of my heart. The only regret I didn't have. I need to be here to see him grow. Ward off the scheming chicks like his mama. God I want to live for my son, but I know no matter what, little Eric would be well taken care of. Yassy will make sure he knows I loved him the most, Braxton too for that matter.

It's so hard for me to breathe, my heart's weak, the beep on the machine is slowing. This pain is tremendous. I hear the sobs from mommy, daddy, Yassy, Kevin, even Braxton. I really try to concentrate on them, but this pain is excruciating. It's willing me to let go. As I let go, rest becomes easier, my pain gradually dissipating.

I hear mommy sobbing, daddy vowing to make Eric pay. I feel my body slipping away. I can barely hear them now. I feel like letting go. I feel the pain freeing as my body drifts further. Eric Ayers, the one who tried to take all my pain, the one who told me it was okay to love him because he wouldn't hurt me, never lied. I lied to him and continued to hurt him the most. Now, he was paying for my sins. He sits in a jail cell.

Eric was a good guy and I turned him into a monster. Eric, I feel so bad. I'm not saying Eric never would have cheated, but who was I to make that call. I never gave him all of me. I sent him mixed signals and definitely drove him crazy along the way. Truth, I went into this relationship, all of my relationships with one goal, make it all about Landon. I did what I had to do to conquer, no repercussions, no intent to love. The relationship was doomed from the beginning. I caused Eric a lot of unwarranted pain. Maybe if I tried, we would have had a relationship where the love was reciprocated. The reality is I will never know, so there was no reason for what ifs. He was warned I would never do him any good. Too often, people do things to prove a point instead of accepting who that person is. They don't pay attention to advice or actions. In Eric's case, he did just that. He tried to prove a point only to hurt himself in the end. I know it wasn't that simple, his heart was vested. I do take a lot of the blame, but I said it before, my attitude did not change with "I do." It was always there. He ignored it.

I should have let him go. He should have took heed, faced the facts. While he was who I needed, I was not who he needed. All he wanted was for me to trust him, let him in. He promised he would never hurt me and he kept his promise. Bottom line, Eric was my scapegoat, savior in a sense. To him, I was a horrible wife. I didn't appreciate the man or title. Loving me was his downfall.

I heard before that hearing is the last function that goes when death comes. It must be true. I don't feel my heart beating, or the movement of my chest going up and down. I hear the heart machine making a long beeeeeeeeeeeep signaling I was gone.

I can't die. God save me. I had to at least do one good thing. I owed Eric so much. It's not right for me to just die while he's in jail. He doesn't deserve this, he didn't belong there. I have to set the record straight. Let them know.....

Eric DID NOT pull the trigger.

It's not over… Fourth installment coming soon.....